A MEETING OF MINDS

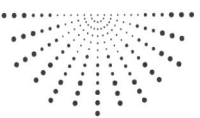

SAM SHORT

Copyright © 2017 by Sam Short

All rights reserved.

No part of this book may be reproduced in any form or by any electronic or mechanical means, including information storage and retrieval systems, without written permission from the author, except for the use of brief quotations in a book review.

❦ Created with Vellum

For my Family. I love you all.

ALSO BY SAM SHORT

Under Lock and Key

Four and Twenty Blackbirds

An Eye For An Eye

CHAPTER ONE

*G*ladys Weaver peeped through the battlements at the top of the castle's tallest tower. She peeped, because even on tip-toe it was a struggle to gain the height she needed to watch her fiancée frolicking in the wildflowers next to the crystal-clear lake, far below.

The strong breeze, funnelled by the mountain valley which cradled Huang Towers, barely moved a hair in her neat blue rinse perm, but it did make the vertigo she seemed to be suffering from a little bit worse. Gladys wouldn't admit to anybody that she had a problem with heights. Not until hell froze over — or her fear became a real obstacle and she was *forced* to admit her failings.

As far as everyone she cared for was concerned, Gladys Weaver feared nothing. Apart from large fires of course, but that was to be expected after very recently being burnt alive. Gladys hated that term – *burnt alive.* She was certain beyond doubt that she had been burnt *to death*. She knew that, because her fiancée had used powerful magic to bring her back *from* death. That, and the fact that her granddaughter, Penny, had described in vivid detail how Gladys's eyes had melted from her skull, and the petite jawline she'd always been so proud of had been charred and devoid of skin and muscle.

Gladys had seen a bright light at the end of a tunnel during the moments she was dead, but she'd kept that particular detail to herself. Had she seen the friendly smiling faces of people at the end of the tunnel, she may have shared her revelation, but Gladys couldn't be bothered with trying to explain why, at the end of her tunnel, she'd seen a grinning monkey juggling with coconuts.

She put it down to her synapses firing wildly as she passed over — she hated to think it might have been her version of hell — a punishment for the time she'd had a tiny mishap while on holiday in Belize. She hadn't aimed the coconut *at* the monkey, the sea-breeze had taken it off course. Anyway, the monkey shouldn't have taken liberties with her bodily parts. Just because a woman chooses to sunbathe nude on a beach does not mean she is hanging out an invitation to groping monkeys. The monkey had made a full recovery anyway, and Gladys had been shamefully escorted from the beach by two burly hotel security guards. She didn't think it fair that the monkey was waiting in hellfire for her.

She didn't worry about hell too much. Death would never come for Gladys again. Not while she was in the dimension known as The Haven. She could die in an accident of course, but no illness would bother her, or any other resident of the magical land. She made sure to take extra care when she went back to the mortal world, though. Wickford may have been a small rural English canal town, but even chocolate box towns had their fair share of dangerous drivers who could snuff out her immortality in an instant.

Gladys smiled as she gazed down at her fiancée. She knew the bush he was nibbling on had thick thorns protruding from the woody stems, and she knew she'd be required to cast a healing spell over his torn lips before he drank his bedtime hot chocolate mixed with brandy. That didn't bother her. It was nice to feel needed sometimes — just as long as he didn't become *too* needy. Neediness was a disease as bad as, if not worse than, scurvy, and if Charleston ever began displaying the tell-tale symptoms, Gladys would put him in his place quicker than her daughter could shovel a plate of snacks down her throat. And that was quick. Very quick.

Charleston Huang had stolen Granny's heart in a matter of weeks, and she couldn't wait to be his wife. Not because he'd promised her the *very* important title of Lady Huang, or that she was excited about being married to the man who possessed the strongest magic in The Haven *and* ruled the realm. Perish the thought. No, Gladys couldn't wait to be his wife because she'd been lonely since her first husband had choked to death on a whole brazil nut. Mostly.

Gladys had convinced herself that it meant that Norman, rest his soul, had suffered from a nut allergy, and she'd long ago given up arguing with people who said otherwise. Her husband's lips had been blue, and his face swollen after the nut had blocked his windpipe — if that wasn't a symptom of anaphylactic shock, she didn't know *what* was.

Gladys waved. "Cooooeee!" she shouted, forcing herself higher on her toes.

Her fiancée ignored her, far too focused on nibbling leaves to pay her any heed. He was a handsome man, Gladys conceded. Of Chinese origin, and in his late sixties, he was over a decade younger than Gladys. That didn't bother either of them though, age was just a number, and their blossoming romance had been a meeting of minds and not a physical attraction.

Her first marriage had *totally* been based on physical attraction. Gladys had first spotted Norman, rest his soul, as he'd hurled insults at the crowd of protestors she was a part of. He'd been standing outside a pub with a crowd of men, booing the protestors, and calling them a *bunch of crazy cat women.* They weren't crazy cat women at all, although at the time Gladys *had* owned two cats, *and* attended weekly anger management courses. But crazy, they were not. They were proud feminists, protesting the patriarchy and the vile way in which women were treated as sex objects in the workplace.

Norman, rest his soul, had caught Gladys's attention as he'd sipped his pint of beer and laughed at the signs her fellow feminists had carried. His shoulder length hair had been luscious and black, and the leather jacket and jeans he wore had made him look somehow… dangerous. Gladys liked danger, and the way Norman, rest his soul, paid no attention to oncoming motor vehicles as he stepped into the road and tossed his empty glass at the protestors, made her sweat. Or glow, she should have said. Women glowed, men perspired and horses sweated — and Gladys was *certainly* not male, or a filly.

The moment the protest had finished, Gladys had rushed home, changed out of her A-line skirt, and wriggled into the shortest mini-skirt she'd owned, tidied her beehive, and applied her make-up liberally. Twenty minutes later she was in the same pub she'd spotted Norman, rest his soul, outside, and half an hour after that, she'd secured herself an invitation to a night out at the cinema with him. The rest was history, and now a new chapter in her life had been opened.

It would have been strange if her attraction to Charleston Huang had been based on physical attributes. She'd hardly seen the man while they were getting to know each other, only venturing once a week into the guest bedroom where his magically frozen body had been propped up in a corner — and those visits were only so she had been able to comb his hair and polish his fancy diamond ring.

During the weeks she'd fallen for him, the man Gladys was soon to be marrying had been trapped in the body of a goat, and if Gladys had felt any physical attraction towards a farm animal, she would have marched herself off to a shrink and demanded he, or preferably she, get to the root of her problems immediately.

The goat incident had all been a very complicated

business, and in the six months since Gladys and Charleston had taken up residency in the castle, Gladys had been forced to tell the story repeatedly to the visitors who insisted on coming to heap praise on Charleston for saving The Haven from an evil witch-finder. Nobody thanked Gladys, and that made her seethe. She was the one who'd made the ultimate sacrifice while Charleston, as she'd been informed after being resurrected, had pranced around shooting magic laser beams from his shiny ring. The ring on his finger, that was.

Tired of repeating the same story to visitors, Gladys had erected a sign next to the main entrance into the castle. She'd erected two in fact, but after taking advice from her daughter, Maggie, she'd taken the first one down and promptly erected the second.

The first one had been concise and to the point.

We, the residents of Huang Towers, are not perverted sex people. If you see Charleston crawling around on all fours and eating grass, it is NOT because we are living out a sexual fetish fantasy. In no way whatsoever! That would just be weird.
Thank you. Your understanding in this matter is appreciated.
Gladys Weaver (soon to be Lady Gladys Huang.)

Gladys had been forced to admit that it did, as Maggie had argued, send out the wrong message. Neither did it explain why Charleston could occasionally be seen on all fours. Penny had been correct too, when she'd said it seemed that the sign protested the couple's innocence a little too much. There was no smoke without fire, she'd noted.

The second sign *was* better, even Gladys could see that.

Do not worry about Charleston if he is on all fours. He isn't drunk, poorly, or playing the fool. I accidentally trapped him in the body of a goat named Boris for a period of time. After breaking the spell, we both agreed that it had been fun while Charleston was a goat, so upon occasion, Charleston likes to magic his mind back into the body of the goat, and the goat's mind will therefore occupy his body – hence his penchant for eating shrubs and toileting outside. Please don't ask questions about it. It's very rude. Thank you. Your unconditional understanding in this matter is demanded.

P.S – Please do not feed Charleston while his body contains the mind of a goat. He will eat anything, and I don't find podgy men attractive.

Gladys Weaver (soon to be Lady Gladys Huang.)

A MEETING OF MINDS

Gladys watched a triangle of geese fly overhead until the clip-clop of hooves on stone drew her attention. She turned to see Boris emerging onto the towertop, his tongue hanging from his mouth and his breath coming in ragged gasps. "Those steps will be the death of me," he panted. "They don't think about goats when they build staircases."

Gladys sighed. "Spend less time as a goat then, Charleston," she said. "In fact, I forbid you from swapping bodies until we're married."

The goat bared his yellowed teeth. "You forbid me?" he said, sitting on his haunches as gained some control over his breathing. "This castle is named after me — Huang Towers. *I'll* be doing any forbidding which happens around here, and *I* forbid *you* from watering my brandy down. I'm not stupid, I can taste tainted liquor from a mile off. It tastes like a cat has micturated in it."

Gladys thought she knew what he meant. Charleston's Oxford education ensured his vocabulary was far in advance of hers, but she liked to try and pretend she understood the big words he used. In this case, the context made it simpler.

She pushed her purple glasses higher up her nose, and raised an eyebrow in the way she'd seen learned men do as they delivered lectures. "I'm not going to ask how you know what cat wizz tastes like…" she paused. The goat didn't contradict her, so she gave herself an imaginary high-five, and continued, "… but I'm doing it for your own good — only until we're married. Then you can get totally leathered every night for all I care. I'm putting my foot down, Charleston. No getting *too* drunk, or being a goat until we're husband and wife. It's only six days, I'm sure you'll manage."

Charleston sighed. "I can do that for you, Gladys. Although you must promise to be on your best behaviour too. I don't want you causing any trouble tonight."

Gladys didn't cause trouble. She responded to it, but she ignored the verbal assault levelled at her, choosing to take the moral high ground instead. There was a very nice view from up there, and she was rarely joined by anybody else who would ruin the seclusion. "Okay," she said, fingers crossed on both hands. "I promise. I'll be on my best behaviour. Now, go and change out of your goat and into something a little smarter. The guests will be arriving soon, and I don't want you putting a hoof in the punch bowl."

CHAPTER TWO

The grand hall was as splendid as the name suggested, and the crowd which filled it was equally as impressive. Huge trolls clutched flagons of mead, and a group of dwarfs stood next to the long buffet table, admiring the ice sculpture which Gladys had conjured into existence with her own fingertips. The huge stallion had begun to melt around the tail area, but the two figures on its back were still in one frozen piece. Charleston's chiselled ice abdominals reflected the lights from the chandeliers, and Gladys's transparent breasts still held their form, the *very* rude areas hidden by petals which cascaded from the rose clenched between her teeth. It was a masterpiece indeed, and the dwarf who was attempting to toss olives into Charleston's mouth, fiercely agape in a battle-cry, would pay a heavy price if Gladys ever met him down a dark alley.

Gladys stared at the guests from the top of the sweeping marble staircase — which would make her entrance as magnificent as the dress she wore. With no magic involved in its making, the hand tailored outfit finally made her feel like the person she'd always known she was.

The importance of the gold thread which held the panels of silvery silk together, complimented the arrogance of the pearl buttons which ran from her neckline to her navel. She knew with one glance across the crowd that she'd stolen the show before she'd even been announced to the guests.

Gladys lifted a glove clad hand in the monarchical greeting she'd been practising before bed each night, but the band continued to play. With an impatient sigh, she took a few steps back from the staircase, and tried again, this time making herself known with a loud shout. "I'm here!" she screeched. "Look at me!"

A group of witches at the bottom of the staircase heard her, and lifted their silver goblets in greeting, but apart from those irrelevant witches, nobody else paid her any notice. The fiddler fiddled faster, and the drummer pounded out a tight beat which people danced to, totally oblivious that the lady of the moment had arrived. *The bride to be was in the room*, yet people were more interested in the debauched mating ritual of the dance-floor than complimenting her on her impeccable dress sense.

Either Gladys's dander was rising, or she'd put on a few pounds since the final dress fitting. Her stomach tightened beneath the fabric and her face warmed with rage, and it was only the appearance of her two granddaughters at the foot of the staircase which prevented her casting a spell which would have put a quick, and possibly fiery, ending to the pre-wedding cocktail and finger foods party.

"Hi Granny!" said Willow, the short black dress she wore tightly wrapping her voluptuous figure.

"You look amazing, Granny," said Penny, her less shapely figure hidden by a looser dress.

Gladys was proud of them both. Even the frumpy one. The girls were beautiful, boasting the same long black hair and bright green eyes — which the girls insisted on calling emerald, although Gladys likened the hue to moss, rather than a precious jewel. They were the girl's eyes, though, and Gladys's honed instincts told her she shouldn't bring any attention to her musings on their eye colour. She would honour the emerald fallacy, and never bring it up. Unless really pushed.

"Girls," said Gladys, gliding down the stairs in much the same manner the heroines did in the black and white movies she was such a fan of. "I'm glad you could make it."

Penny moved with speed, catching Gladys in her arms and preventing her from falling any further. "Don't lift your knees so high when you walk in heels," she said, "take smaller steps."

"You looked like you were goose stepping," said Willow.

The youngest ones were always the rudest.

Gladys adjusted her tiara, and scowled. "I was floating, Willow. Like in the movies."

"Oh, right," said Willow, "well float your way down the rest of the staircase more carefully. Marble can be very slippery."

Penny and Willow each took one of Gladys's elbows in a hand, helping her navigate the remainder of the stairs and steering her through the crowd at the base.

"Mum and everyone else can't wait to see you," said Penny, squeezing past a troll, and smiling at one of the fairy waitresses which her grandmother had insisted on employing for the event.

The fairies may have been small, but they possessed a great strength which enabled them to effortlessly carry trays laden with drinks, zooming high above the crowd instead of struggling through it like a terrestrial waitress would have been forced to.

All thoughts of punishing the crowd for failing to acknowledge her arrival vanished as Gladys spotted a bright red jacket, barely containing the spherical belly beneath it. "Brian!" she shouted, "my son! You came!"

Brian stopped spinning the little umbrella he held, and slid it into his bright green cocktail, placing the glass on a table. "Of course I came, Mother!" he gushed. "I wouldn't have missed it for all the tulips in Amsterdam!" He grabbed Gladys in a fierce hug. "The ice sculpture is amazing by the way, a pure masterpiece, and you look fabulous — like a fairy-tale queen!"

"You look fantastic too," said Gladys, taking a step backwards and looking her son up and down. The red jacket *was* perfectly lovely — most definitely his colour. *As if Brian would ever be seen wearing anything that wasn't!* Gladys did have her reservations about the black leather trousers, though. Surely her son would sweat… she caught herself mid-thought… *perspire,* as he made beautiful shapes on the dance floor, and surely that would lead to dehydration which could lead to… Gladys scolded herself and calmed her beating heart. They were in The Haven — of course her first born wasn't going to drop dead in the middle of the band's version of YMCA! He was protected by magic. Gladys gave her son the lop-sided smile which was firmly reserved for him. "You look magnificent!"

Gladys jumped as she became aware of a large colourful shape to her right. She recoiled for a moment, concerned it was a randy troll overcome by her beauty, but smiled when she saw the chubby face of her daughter. "Maggie, you look… bright," she said.

Her daughter wore a shapeless dress, printed with colourful flowers and tied at the waist with a belt. She clutched a sandwich in her hand, and not for the first time, Gladys wondered just how fatter a thumb could become before it was no longer opposable.

Maggie took a bite of her sandwich. "I'd have looked a lot nicer if it wasn't for Charleston's stupid spell," she complained.

The spell which Charleston had placed over Huang Towers, and for a fifty-mile radius around it, was an understandable precaution, in Gladys's opinion. It prevented witches and wizards from being able to revert to a younger age — a gift bestowed upon them when they first entered The Haven. After recent

A MEETING OF MINDS

events, when an evil Witch-finder had misused the gift to hide himself amongst the residents of the magical land, Charleston had thought it prudent to protect against such wicked use of magic in the future. Maggie was just annoyed that she couldn't shift into her younger body, although in Gladys's opinion, her daughter looked better in her forties than she had as a teenager. Her acne had been terrible back then, and Gladys was sure her thighs had been thicker.

"The spell is sensible," said Gladys, looking around the room. "Anyway, where is Charleston? He was supposed to announce me when I made my entrance. I looked quite the fool at the top of that staircase. That man had better not be such a let-down when we're married."

"He's with Barney," said Penny. "They're having a cigar together outside."

"Charleston's got Barney on the cigars?" said Gladys. "I'll kill him! Your boyfriend's body is far too frail for him to risk becoming a smoker. Does he even have any lungs in that tiny pigeon chest of his?"

Penny pursed her lips in the way she did when she was trying to keep words in her mouth. That was one of the main differences between her granddaughters –

Willow didn't know when to shut up, and Penny didn't speak up enough.

"He's having one cigar, Granny," said Penny, her narrowed eyes communicating what she *really* wanted to say. "It won't kill him."

"And Barney has not got a pigeon chest," said Willow, standing beside her older sister. "Don't be so rude. It's just that he's so tall."

Gladys didn't need telling how tall Barney was. The ginger-haired policeman towered over Penny, and Gladys often wondered if anyone else had a nickname for the couple like the one she had. *Stumpy and Lanky* wasn't a particularly rude pet name for the odd pair, but Gladys kept it safely locked away in the part of her brain labelled *insults for a rainy day* — Penny could be highly sensitive, and since being promoted to the rank of Sergeant, Barney had become less tolerant of Gladys's highly tuned sense of humour. It was safer that Gladys kept it to herself until the day it was needed to win an argument.

"I don't like to think of him puffing on cigars," said Gladys. "He's a mortal. He's not protected by magic like Charleston is."

"The lad will be fine," said Brian. "Anyway, Mother, I think it's about time me and you had a dance. The band are very good indeed, it's a shame you can't bring them to Wickford for your wedding reception. They'd bring the roof down."

Technically, the band *could* travel to Wickford. It would have been difficult in the past, but since Charleston had taken charge of The Haven, he'd implemented some changes. Gladys's favourite was the inclusion of a permanent portal to Wickford, which opened in the potting shed at the bottom of her cottage garden in Wickford, right next to the coop where her chickens had lived before being transported to Huang Towers with the rest of her most personal of effects.

Witches and wizards could still open their own portals into The Haven, but Huang Towers boasted a portal room through which *anyone* could pass, mortal or magic. Portal technicalities weren't the reason the band couldn't play at the wedding reception in Wickford — the problem was more aesthetic. Gladys didn't think the residents of Wickford, who had no idea that witches walked among them, would take kindly to watching a troll thumping a drum, accompanied by a fairy on vocals. It would cause more problems than Gladys wanted to deal with on her special day.

The wedding was to be an ordinary event, in the mortal world, with mortal guests. The only witches present would be her own family, and they knew better than to use magic in the presence of normal people.

"I'd love to dance!' said Gladys, taking the hand Brian offered her and allowing herself to be led onto the dance-floor.

The music reminded Gladys of the festivals she'd attended in the sixties, and she twirled and bobbed next to her son, ignoring the jealous stares of the other dancers. Yes, she was dancing with the most handsome man in the room, and yes, her dress was far classier than anybody else's, but there was never an excuse for envy. Gladys was happy that she'd never been held in the evil grip of the green-eyed monster. She shuddered as she imagined what it must feel like to covet what other people had.

Brian danced faster as the music increased in tempo, lifting his legs remarkably high for such a stout fellow wearing tight leather trousers. Gladys took a deep breath. She couldn't keep up. How could she? Her son was a fertile fountain of energy, and she was in her… well, she was older. It would have been an affront to her pride to admit she couldn't match her son's energy, though. She needed a way out — an excuse to leave the dance-floor while keeping her dignity intact.

Gladys peeped between the writhing bodies on the dance-floor. And then she saw it. If there was one thing Gladys hated more than anything else, it was oppression. She called it out wherever she found it, and to see it happening at her own party filled her with rage. It was a personal insult to her, and her wrath would be swift and fearsome when she found out who was responsible for the despicable scene unfolding in the corner.

Having found the perfect excuse to leave the dance-floor, Gladys barged through the crowd, shouting an apology to her son over her shoulder. "Have a cocktail, sweetheart! I have to deal with something. I'm sure Maggie would love to dance with you when she's finished eating!"

Magic tingled in her belly, and her fingertips sizzled with energy as she poised herself in readiness cast a spell. Brian would have to wait until later to dance with his sister — Gladys required everyone's full attention as she saved the unfortunate soul in the corner from his oppressor. People needed to be made aware. It was the only way society could heal.

The spell buzzed in the air around her, and Gladys's throat quivered as her vocal chords were imbued with voice amplification magic. She put a hand on the poor dwarf's shoulder and gave him a reassuring look. "Don't worry," she soothed. "I'm here now. Nobody will ever do this to you again."

The dwarf seemed tense, and Gladys had enough empathy to realise why. The poor little chap had been humiliated, and that simply wasn't acceptable. Not in the current year.

Gladys took a deep breath and allowed the magic to collect in her throat before casting her voice in a powerful wave of sound. "Stop the music! Everybody look over here. Look at this poor dwarf!" she yelled. The crystal chandelier hanging above the dance-floor shook as she shouted, her voice a reverberating foghorn propelled by magic. A fairy waitress, hit by the shockwave, dropped her tray and tumbled from the air, saving herself from the hard floor with a frantic flapping of her silvery wings.

"Gladys, what's wrong?" said a voice to her right.

Good. Charleston had decided to make an appearance. She could really show off with him watching her.

"I'll tell you what's wrong!" said Gladys, speaking to the room. "Somebody thought it was funny to put this dwarf on a high bar stool! That's what's wrong! Look, his tiny feet are dangling in the air, the poor, poor chap!" Gladys plucked the dwarf from the stool, and tenderly placed him on the floor, acutely aware that he was blushing. *How could anybody do that to him?* "And look at the flagon he's been given for his beer!" she continued. "He can barely get his baby fingers around it. Somebody get him a beaker more appropriate to his size, and fetch him a chair that will fit his stumpy little legs! When I find out who did this, there'll be hell to play!"

The dwarf licked bubbles of beer froth from his bushy moustache and looked up at Gladys. "This is very embarrassing."

Gladys stood tall. "Did you all hear that?" she boomed. "He's embarrassed! I hope whoever thought it was funny to put him on that stool is ashamed of themselves!" She bent at the waist and stared the dwarf in the eyes. "Who did this to you? Point whoever it was out to me, and I'll make sure you'll never be so humiliated again."

"I got up there myself," said the dwarf. "I'm not disabled."

"A good thing too," said Gladys. "That would have made it immeasurably worse." She ended the voice amplification spell and put her lips close to the dwarf's ear, barely preventing herself from sneezing as coarse hair tickled her nostrils. "You're not a grass, I get it, and that's very admirable. Nobody likes a grass, but if you change your mind, you come and tell me who did it to you."

"Come on, Gladys," said Charleston, putting a hand on her shoulder. "Leave him alone. Let's dance. You've got a big day tomorrow, you don't want to spend the night worrying about other people."

Charleston was right. He always was. Thinking of others was her Achilles heel. She knew that, and she had to remind herself to focus on *her* more often. Anyway, she'd garnered the attention she craved for the night, and she *did* have a big day tomorrow. She was visiting Wickford to make the final arrangements for her wedding. She had a band to book for her reception, a cake to check on, and an organ player to choose.

It would be a difficult choice. Both organists were very adept, and both seemed very keen to get the gig. It was going to be the wedding of the millennia after all, no wonder they seemed so competitive.

Charleston had argued that the women's competitiveness was a reaction to the amount of money Gladys was offering for their services. She'd asked for a rendition of *Here Comes the Bride* to be played as she walked down the aisle, and a few bars of *Elton John's — Rocket Man*, as the newlyweds left the chapel. She didn't think two-thousand-pounds was a gross overpayment, as Charleston had argued. It was obvious to Gladys that the reason both women desperately wanted the gig was not financially motivated, it was so the winner could boast that they'd been a part of the classiest wedding service the small town had ever seen.

Deep down, Gladys suspected that Ethel already had the gig in the bag. Her fingers were a lot slenderer than Mavis's, and her hair far shinier. Gladys would be *very* surprised if Mavis was two-grand up on Saturday. She'd find out tomorrow though, when she asked them both to play in the chapel she'd chosen to get married in.

Gladys put her hand on the dwarf's head and gave his hair an affectionate rub. He was still blushing, and she wasn't surprised. Goddess only knew how long he'd been stuck on the stool. She nodded at the band. "Play!" she ordered, watching in amazement as the dwarf scrambled back onto the stool and picked up his beer. "The night is still young!"

CHAPTER THREE

When Gladys had arrived in her potting shed, the portal closing with a popping sound behind her, she'd set about doing some housework in her cottage. She may not have been living there anymore, but it was still her home, and she was nothing if not house-proud. She wouldn't use magic to get the task done either – where was the pride in that?

With the dusting finished and the vacuuming completed, she set about walking into Wickford. The bright sun lit the narrow country lane which led her into town, and it wasn't long before she was on High Street, making her way towards the canal. Penny and Willow were waiting for her on the boat they called their home. Gladys had asked for their help in picking between the two organists, and they'd been happy to help. Or so they'd said.

Gladys was half way down High Street when she heard the noise. She scurried across the road to see what all the commotion was about, pushing through the small crowd which had gathered in front of the Post Office.

"Shut up with that racket, I'm trying to get slaughtered on cider here!"

Gladys frowned at the tramp. Wickford had certainly gone downhill if they allowed hobos to drink cider in the street. The busker that the tramp was shouting at tried his best to ignore the outburst, but Gladys could see the frustration etched on his face as he angrily strummed his guitar.

The music he played wasn't a *racket* by any stretch of the imagination, in fact, Gladys found the music right up her street. It was a pleasing soundtrack to accompany her morning stroll, and the man's voice was as soft as the butter which Gladys had spread on her crumpets that morning.

The crowd of people began to wander away as the tramp continued his outburst, some of them muttering under their breath. "Will you shut up!" the hobo yelled, this time reinforcing his words with the toss of a well-aimed empty can, which bounced off the busker's full head of curls and landed on the pavement.

Gladys cracked her knuckles, but reminded herself that performing magic was a no-no in the middle of Wickford High Street. Her tongue would have to suffice in her delivery of the hobo's chastisement. "That's enough of that, you violent little blighter!" she shouted. "That young man is trying to make something of himself, you, on the other hand, are a nasty piece of work!"

The drunk man scowled at Gladys. "Shut up, you nosy old boot, or you'll get a can on your bonce too!"

Gladys had nothing against the homeless. She found them to be a brave and resilient sort of person, most of them with higher morals than the richest of bankers. She'd often thrown a coin or two into a hat in the past, but the only thing the man who sat on the pavement at her feet was going to receive, was the business end of her arm if he wasn't careful.

The tramp stared up at her. "What you looking at?" he taunted, using a dirty hand to shield his eyes from the sun, and drawing his tongue across the top of his long, matted beard.

Gladys bent down and adjusted her eyebrows into high arches as she peered over her spectacles. With her face fixed in the expression which had once made her children run for the stairs, she spoke slowly and clearly. "I don't know who you think you are, or what you think you're doing, but I swear by all that is good, if you don't stand up right this very moment, walk away, and crawl back under whatever stone you slid out from beneath, I will make you sorry that you ever crossed me."

The man opened his mouth to speak, but sensibly thought better of it. Silently, he placed his cans of cider in a plastic bag, stood up, gave Gladys a nervous frown, and wobbled off down the street, scowling at the busker as he pushed past him. He looked over his shoulder and gave a parting statement. "I didn't crawl out from under a stone — it's more of a rock."

"Well hurry up back there!" said Gladys. "The other creatures will be missing you!"

The busker sighed. "Thank you," he said. "I'm trying to earn enough money to fix my car, but he's been scaring people off all morning, and I don't like confrontation."

"No thanks are necessary, young man," said Gladys. "I won't stand for rudeness like that from anybody." She opened her purse and took out a handful of coins. "Here," she said, dropping them in the little box at the busker's feet. "You play beautifully."

The busker smiled his appreciation, and twisted one of the guitar's tuning pegs. "Can I play something for you? Name your favourite tune. I'd be happy to oblige."

"Anything?" said Gladys, her eyes sparkling as an idea formed. "Can you play *Wichita Lineman*?"

"Of course," said the busker, adjusting his fingers of the neck of the guitar. "It's one of my favourites."

That was enough for Gladys. Anybody who shared her highly refined taste in music was worthy of her help. "How much will your car cost to repair, young man?" she said, before the busker had time to strike the first chord. "And have you got friends who can play with you? I'm looking for a band."

The busker scratched his head. "Urm… I'm not sure about the cost of the car, but I'm in a band, yes. We're called *The Blanket Statement*."

"Would four-thousand-pounds cover the car?" asked Gladys. "Because if it would, and if you're free on Saturday night, I'd be happy to offer you a gig at a wedding party. I'd pay each of you four grand of course, if the rest of the band are as good as you."

Since taking up residency in The Haven, money had become no barrier to Gladys. Gold was abundant in the magical dimension, and Gladys had secured herself a precious metal broker in the mortal world, who would happily take it off her hands for a fair price. She needed to be careful though. The first broker she'd approached had phoned the police when Gladys had told him she had as much gold as he could take off her hands, and then some more.

The police couldn't *really* bother Gladys. She could spend all her time in The Haven if she liked, but she didn't want the stigma which surrounded being a wanted person in the mortal world, so she only sold gold when her bank account balance dropped below thirty-thousand-pounds, which seemed like a nice round number to her. The bank she used had never questioned her cash deposits, and if they ever did, she'd cast a spell and shut them the heck up. *Nosy buggers*.

She enjoyed spreading her wealth with people who deserved it, and seeing the busker's eyes light up was reward enough for being thousands of pounds lighter.

"Of course," stammered the busker. "I'd be happy to, but that much money… really?"

"Yes, really," smiled Gladys. She looked the young man up and down, his jeans and t-shirt ensemble was acceptable for a street performance, but not for a performance at *her* wedding. "Six o'clock — in The Poacher's Pocket Hotel, next to the canal, and make sure you all wear something smart. I'll pay you on the night."

"Thank you…"

"Gladys Weaver," said Gladys, accepting the busker's handshake.

"Thomas Ericson," said the young man. "And I'll make sure it's the best show the band have ever put on."

"I have the upmost trust in you," said Gladys.

Gladys left Thomas looking very happy with himself, and headed for the bakery. With the band arranged so quickly, Gladys was sure the day was going to go as smoothly as she'd expected it would. Good luck seemed to stalk her, and finding Thomas singing in High Street was good luck indeed. All she had left to do was check on the cake and pick an organist for the church. Simple, just how she liked things.

THE SUN SPARKLED on the water, and the bright reds and greens of the paintwork that decorated Penny's boat stood out beautifully against the lush foliage of the canal bank. Gladys had been adamant that she wanted to arrive at the bank-side chapel on her wedding day aboard *The Water Witch*. She was fed up of seeing brides arriving at their weddings in horse drawn carriages or long-past-it classic cars. She thought it was about time somebody made a stand against tradition.

Today would not only be about choosing an organist, but would also give Penny a trial run at mooring the boat in the correct position next to the chapel. Canal narrowboats were very long, and the wooden pier which Gladys wanted to step off the boat onto was very narrow. She didn't want to suffer the indignity of having to wait while Penny reversed and tried again on the day of her wedding. If she didn't pull off the perfect mooring procedure on the first time she attempted it today, there would be no second chance — Gladys had already decided that, if required, she'd use a spell on the day of the ceremony to ensure the smoothest of aquatic arrivals.

Gladys gazed around the mooring. Her granddaughters were sitting at one of the two picnic benches on the bank-side, drinking tea, but apart from Penny's cat, Rosie, and the birds in the tree tops, there were no other animals to be seen. "No Mabel?" she said, slightly disappointed.

Mabel was a goose which had suffered at the hands of Gladys's witch dementia. When a spell had gone awry, it had made the goose believe she was a dog. It had been fun watching the goose cock its leg while it went to the toilet, and her barking had certainly been a talking point in the town. When Gladys's dementia had been cured, all her accidental spells had been reversed at the same time, the most important one being the freeing of Charleston's mind from the body of a goat.

"She visits now and again," said Penny. "She's still got a taste for bacon rind, and she still enjoys playing with Rosie."

"And she still chases swans," said Willow, patting the bench next to her. "Sit down, Granny." She lifted the red knitted cozy from the teapot. "Tea?" she asked. "It's your favourite, Earl Grey."

Gladys shook her head impatiently, and looked at her watch. "No, and I told you I wanted to be leaving by ten o'clock. I'd have thought the boat engine would have been running by now and you'd both be ready to pipe me aboard."

"It will only take twenty minutes to get to the chapel, Granny," said Penny, "and the organists aren't due there until half-past eleven. You've got time for a cup of tea."

Gladys held her tongue, but visibly bristled. Young people these days seemed to possess no sense of urgency. She liked to arrive for appointments early, and anyway, she'd told the girls she wanted to spend some time assessing the condition of the small chapel. It had been unused for two decades, and she'd paid the horrible farmer who owned the land it was built on a pretty penny for the old building.

She enjoyed owning a chapel, as decrepit as it was, and she was looking forward to conjuring an organ into existence inside it. Since her witch dementia had been cured, Gladys was itching to use as much magic as possible, and was planning on casting a beautifying spell over the chapel on the night before her wedding.

Her family had attempted to persuade her to get married elsewhere, telling her there were far nicer places available, but her parents had tied the knot in that chapel, and Gladys's mother always did have good taste. Her parents had loved each other dearly, and Gladys's mother had turned down her chance of immortality in The Haven, to be buried alongside her mortal husband in the Wickford church cemetery. She wanted to honour them by saying her vows in the same spot they'd said theirs.

She still felt guilty about her first marriage.

Gladys had married Norman in the church *his* mother had wanted to see her son married in, forcing Gladys's mother to put aside her wishes to see the wedding happen in the little canal-side chapel, but now Gladys could finally make amends.

Gladys considered the teapot for a moment. "No time for tea," she said, folding her arms.

Penny stood up and gathered the teapot and cups together, placing them on a tray. "Come on then, Granny," she said, climbing aboard *The Water Witch*. "We'll get you to the church on time."

CHAPTER FOUR

Gladys loved *The Water Witch*. She loved the smell inside the narrow interior when the girls cooked on the gas stove, and she loved the potted herbs and flowers which grew on the flat roof. There was something lovely about travelling along a narrow English canal in a colourful floating home, and she occasionally envied the lifestyle of the girls.

She didn't like the noise of the diesel engine, though, or the vibrations it made which shook their way up her calf muscles as she stood on the stern — or was it bow — decking with her granddaughters. She remembered what Penny had told her — think about which end you'd put a ribbon *bow* on if you wanted to make the boat look pretty Gladys thought it much easier to refer to the two extremities of the boat as the pointy end, and the noisy end.

Knowing she was on the stern decking made no difference to her enjoyment of the short journey. Engine annoyances aside, Gladys revelled in her surroundings, laughing at the ducks which flapped out of the boats path, and taking deep sniffs of the wild garlic as they passed ancient woodland.

When Penny let her take control of the boat, Gladys made sure to remain within the strict speed limit applied by the canal authorities. It was slow going, but so much fun, and Gladys bit her bottom lip as she carefully guided the pointy end into the tiny gap beneath a stone bridge. The walls of the tunnel were so close she could have touched them if she'd wanted, and the musty aroma of wet moss reminded her of childhood adventures in the small cave system which ran beneath the hills surrounding Wickford.

Gladys licked her lips as they passed the Wickford brewery, tasting the mustiness of the hops, and averted her eyes as Lord and Lady Green's mansion came into view. Perched atop a chalk hill, it loomed over the canal, and Gladys wouldn't give the wealthy owners the courtesy of her admiration for their home. Was she jealous, she wondered, but felt better when she reminded herself that Huang Towers was ten times the size of the mansion on the hill. She was better than the Greens were, only in a different dimension.

"Okay," said Penny, as their destination appeared around a bend. "If you want me to prove I can moor the boat in the correct position, you'd better let me take over."

"I'm sure you'll do a fine job," said Gladys, stepping away from the controls. She wasn't sure at all, but she'd give the girl a chance.

Hidden by bank-side trees, the small chapel was not visible to canal traffic, but the small pier could be seen, tucked away where the canal widened into a purpose built mooring.

Gladys imagined the chapel was built to serve as a place for narrowboat crews to say their Sunday prayers during the heyday of the canal system, when coal was transported across Britain by countless boats. She also imagined the crews had spent more time in the pubs and hotels which graced the banks of every canal system in the country.

Penny applied gentle pressure to the steering tiller, nudging the bow closer to the shore. Tugging the power lever backwards, she put the engine into reverse, the propeller viciously churning the water behind them and slowing their progress to a crawl. A gentle thud on the hull was the only indication that the boat was in position.

"I knew you could do it, Penny," said Gladys. "You should have more faith in yourself."

Penny killed the engine and stepped onto the pier, tying the boat off with a short rope. "I really should, shouldn't I?" she said with a smile.

Gladys stepped off *The Water Witch*. The pier was level with the deck of the boat, and it was a simple case of taking a tiny step over the low deck railing onto the jetty. Easy-peasy. The dress she had chosen to be married in was a simple affair, and she envisioned no problems with repeating the debarking procedure on her big day. The creaky old pier would need some sprucing up, but it would be child's play to cast a spell which would do the job.

Willow and Penny walked alongside their grandmother as they followed the footpath which led through the trees. Gladys was happy to see that the path was wide enough for her guests to gather on and watch her as she stepped off the boat. They'd have a fine view of her magnificence as she gracefully stepped ashore.

The little Chapel came into view around the

second small bend in the path, and for the first time since she'd agreed to marry Charleston, Gladys felt a lump in her throat and a tickle in her tummy. She widened her stride and quickened her pace. There was no time for emotion. Emotion was the root of all problems. She was there on business. "Come on girls," she ordered. "Keep up. I want to have a proper look around before Ethel and Mavis arrive, *and* I've got an organ to make out of thin air."

Gladys had taken a cursory glance at the chapel when she'd bought it from the farmer, but she'd not wanted to seem *too* keen, and end up paying above market value. Although money was of no real significance to her any longer, her charitable outlook with her wealth ended at farmer's deep pockets. Since one of their ilk had rejected her romantic advances in the *Coffee Pot Café* in Wickford, Gladys had held a deep disregard for the troublesome bumpkins.

Farmer Bill had *publicly* rejected her, and Gladys had vowed that from that day forward she would remain a widow. Men, particularly farming men, were just too complicated. With her views on men so deeply engrained, it had surprised her as much as everybody else when she'd fallen for Charleston.

Of course, she denied Farmer Bill's claims when her family confronted her about the incident, explaining that she'd simply been reaching into his lap to retrieve some dropped food. She'd had her revenge on Farmer Bill, naturally. She'd poured a magic potion into his dairy herd's drinking trough, which had given the beasts the ability to leap the four-foot high fence which surrounded their field. The rampaging cows had gone on to cause havoc in the town, forcing Farmer Bill to pay for the damage out of his own pocket when his insurers refused to pay out on his claim.

Gladys couldn't remember the complete list of ingredients which had gone into the potion, but she was certain that milk and an energy drink had been involved. Maybe the hind legs of a frog had been included, too.

It didn't take long for the three of them to look around the building. The chapel was a simple structure, consisting of four walls and a doorway beneath a sloping slate roof. The thick walls were built from stone, probably hauled out of the nearby Wickford quarry, and the large door was made from oak, secured to the frame by heavy iron hinges.

Most of the windows were cracked or smashed, but Gladys could see they had once been beautiful stained glass. She would repair them when she cast the beautification spell, as well as repairing the broken pews inside, *and* the weather worn railings which surrounded the chapel. The spell would stay in effect for as long as she wanted it to, and with an additional flexing of her magical muscles she would add a charm to the mix which would make people think it was perfectly normal for a chapel to be derelict one day, and in its former glory the next. She would even be able to stop people wondering why, a day later, it was derelict yet again.

Her guests would have to park their cars alongside the road, a five-minute walk away, but Gladys thought that a short walk was a small price to pay for witnessing her wedding, *and* spending the night eating and drinking for free in the *Poacher's Pocket Hotel*. There was even going to be Pimm's served as the guests arrived at the hotel, for goddess's sake. *They'd better be grateful*.

Gladys led the way inside the chapel, and Penny, ever the pessimist, turned her nose up at the mess. "I wasn't expecting it to be this bad," she said, wiping a finger across a dust laden windowsill.

Willow was more concerned with keeping her clothes clean, and rubbed at a mark on her shorts left by the dirty end of a broken pew. "It's going to take a powerful spell to clean this up," she said.

"You leave that to me," said Gladys. "You won't

recognise this place by the time I'm finished with it." Gladys ignored the mess and marched down the aisle, imagining the admiring glances she'd be attracting when she did it for real — when the seats were full of guests. The more Gladys thought about her wedding day, the more she was becoming excited about the prospect, and she smiled when she saw the perfect position for the organ. It would look splendid placed along the far wall, behind the altar at which she'd say her vows.

She wasn't planning on conjuring up an excessively decorative organ, but she wanted it to have a good set of lungs, and at least a dozen pipes. It needed to be audible all the way from the pier after all, as her guests welcomed her off the boat and joined her in the ceremonial walk along the pathway.

"Watch and learn," said Gladys, cracking her knuckles. "This is going to be a sight to behold." Sparks fizzed at Gladys's fingertips, and she muttered a few words under her breath. The words meant nothing, but she enjoyed showing off. Making a spell seem more difficult than it really was, cemented her position as the most powerful witch in the family.

Her granddaughters were progressing in their understanding of magic, but it would be a long time before one of them could weave the invisible strands of magic in the air into a physical object as technically impressive as an organ. Gladys closed her eyes and imagined what she wanted to create, her stomach tingling and her fingertips warm as magic flowed from them.

"Woah!" said Willow, as a shape began to form against the wall.

The air in the room throbbed as the shape grew larger, and dust vibrated on the floor.

"Amazing," said Penny.

Gladys laughed. "Child's play," she boasted.

Wood and metal twisted in the air, expanding and shimmering as Gladys concentrated. With a flourish of her hand, while she pictured a bull elephant in her mind's eye, the organ's keys began to form, making a tinkling sound as they lined up in their correct positions.

Gladys paused. Mrs Jenkins had an invitation to the wedding, and Gladys was certain she was still a highly vocal activist in PETA. She waved her hand once more, and the ivory keys vanished, immediately replaced by what she assumed was some sort of viable plastic substitute. Gladys forced one last surge of magic from her fingers, and with a final twisting of materials, and a blast of sound from the organ's pipes which made Willow jump, the instrument was complete. Gladys waved her hand once more, and a small stool appeared in front of the instrument, the cushion upholstered in a finely woven silver and gold material.

Penny patted Gladys on her back. "That was cool, granny," she said. "You'll have to teach me that someday."

Gladys smiled at her granddaughters. Standing between them in the very position she was going to say her vows from, reminded her of an honour she'd been meaning to bestow upon them. "Girls." she said. "Don't get too excited, a screech would really echo in this chapel and hurt our ears, but I've got something to tell you both." She paused for dramatic effect, and smiled. "I know I said I wasn't going to have any, but you'll be over the moon to learn that I'm going to allow you to be my bridesmaids, and I'm going to order Maggie to be my maid of honour. Do you think she'd mind wearing a slimming black dress, or would that make her think of funerals?"

"Firstly... thank you," said Penny, although Gladys sensed her appreciation was bogus. "And secondly, don't you dare *ask* Mum to be your maid of honour and then tell her to wear black because it's slimming. That would definitely be in the top ten of a list of the worst things you've ever done."

"I agree," said Willow, frowning. "Top five even, and you've done some terrible things, Granny."

"I'm sorry," said Gladys. "But I disagree. The only way Maggie is going to lose any weight is *by* the rest of us shaming her into doing it. She lost twelve-pounds in a week once, on a family trip to Pontins, and that was *purely* through shame tactics. I followed her around making sounds like a greedy piglet every time she ate something. There were tears at the time, but when she got home she was able to fit into the previous year's school and girl guides uniforms. It saved me and her dad a small fortune. Clothes weren't cheap back then, you see. We didn't have Asian sweatshops knocking out cheap tat — we paid good money for quality goods."

"You did what?" said Willow.

"We paid good money for quality goods," repeated Gladys.

"You *know* I didn't mean that part," said Willow.

"That's really awful," said Penny. "How old was Mum?"

Gladys adjusted her spectacles and looked heavenward. "Let me think… oh yes! Norman, rest his soul, had booked the holiday because…" she lowered her voice, worried the name she was about to utter would be considered sacrilege inside a chapel,

"...*Margaret Thatcher* had just become Prime Minister. We were considering enquiring about refugee status in Canada, but a seven-day all-inclusive break sufficed. That was in nineteen-seventy-nine, so your mother would have been... ten."

Willow's gasp filled the small building. "You evil old bit—"

"Hello!" came a voice from behind them, cutting Willow off mid insult. "I hope I'm not too early, but I do like to be punctual. I notice Ethel's not here yet, I hope she won't be late on your big day if she's given the position of organist. I know *I* wouldn't." The new arrival stared at her surroundings. "It's in a bit of a state, isn't it?" she said. Her eyes lit up when she saw the organ, and she hurried down the aisle flexing her fingers. "But, oh my, what a beautiful piece of craftsmanship. I can't wait to try it out, it must have cost a fortune! I bet it sings like an angel!"

Gladys stared at the woman. Mavis Buttersworth. Gladys had expected a little one-upmanship to be involved in the battle to become her organ grinder, but Mavis had taken it too far. Being early with the intent to impress was one thing, and Gladys respected her for it, but everything else was just wrong. It was sucking up, and Gladys hated a teacher's pet.

Everything from her shiny shoes and posh frock,

to the scent of her fancy perfume, screamed *'pick me!'* The severest of her crimes was on her head though, and Gladys peered over her glasses as she studied it. "New hairdo, Mavis?" she enquired.

"Oh, yes," said Mavis, adjusting the corsage on her flat chest. "Thank you for noticing. It's quite a change for me, but I do love it. I think it's classy. Very classy indeed."

If Gladys had been a nasty woman she would have thrown Mavis out of the chapel right there and then. If Mavis thought emulating Gladys's hairdo would gain her brownie points, she was barking up the wrong tree. Heck – she was barking in the wrong forest completely. Gladys was the only woman in Wickford with a blue rinse perm. Even when they'd gone out of fashion, and the other mature women in town began resembling mutton dressed as lamb with their bleached blonde hair, Gladys had stuck religiously to her tight blue curls.

Mavis had taken a liberty, and Gladys feared that even if Mavis proved to be the better organ player, she wouldn't be able to see past the infraction. The bouncy blue rinse perm was clouding her judgement. If she had the temerity to try and upstage Gladys at an organ playing session, what on earth would she do on the wedding day?

Gladys was about to speak her mind when the second organist arrived.

"Hello," said Ethel, from the doorway. "I hope I'm not late."

"A little," said Mavis. "The early bird catches the worm is the mantra *I* live by."

The damn cheek of that woman made Gladys's toes curl, and if she'd had hackles they'd have been standing fully to attention. "No, Ethel, you're not," she said. "And may I say how wonderful you look? Is that a shell-suit? I haven't seen one of those for years."

"Hmmm," said Mavis. "It's not really suited to such an occasion as this now, is it?"

"I like it. It's very nice," said Willow. "Very lilac."

"Very shiny," added Penny.

"It makes me feel safe. I haven't worn it for a long time, but the last time I did was in this very building," said Ethel, straightening her jacket. "To be honest with you all — I almost didn't come here today. This place brings back a few bad memories."

"You've been here before?" said Penny, moving aside as Ethel approached the organ.

"A long time ago," said Ethel, "but I'd rather not talk about it. I would like to talk about that organ though, it's beautiful. When did you have it installed?"

"Not important. Never mind the irrelevant details," said Granny, tactfully and skilfully steering the conversation in a different direction. "I've got an organist to choose. Let's get this show on the road."

CHAPTER FIVE

"I hope you'll pick wisely," said Mavis. "It is your big day after all, you don't want anything to go wrong, I'm sure."

Gladys resisted the urge to grab Mavis by her admittedly lovely perm, and drag her through the doorway, but she *wanted* Mavis to play. It would be a pleasure to break the news to her that Ethel was the superior player. She'd soon realise that wearing her hair in a snazzy manner would not have any influence over Gladys's opinion.

Gladys clapped. "You play first, Mavis," she said. "Start with *Here Comes The Bride,* please."

Mavis gave a presumptuous grin, misinterpreting Gladys's reasoning behind asking her to go first. Gladys wanted to make sure the organ was nicely warmed up for Ethel, but as Mavis gathered her skirt around her bottom and took a seat in front of the organ, she obviously considered being chosen to play first a compliment. She twiddled with some knobs and did something with her feet, and with an unnecessary tilt of her head to the left, began to play.

The Chapel vibrated with sound, and Penny and Willow clapped as *Here Comes The Bride* boomed from the twelve organ pipes. It did sound good, even Gladys could admit that to herself, and she found herself imagining the walk down the aisle on the arm of her son. A tear threatened to wet her cheek, and Gladys rushed forward and tapped Mavis on the shoulder. "Enough!"

Mavis stopped playing and looked over her shoulder, her pupils dilated and her cheeks red. "It's a beautiful instrument," she said. "One of the best I've played!"

"Keep your knickers on," said Gladys. "Don't get too excited. Let's see how you deal with *Rocket Man*. And be forewarned — if you mess up Elton John's beautiful masterpiece, there'll be no second chance. The rest of us will go outside to listen. I want to make sure the sound will carry on the wind, I want the music to echo through the valley. Don't start playing until I shout the order."

With Mavis's fingers poised over the keyboard,

Penny, Willow and Ethel followed Gladys from the chapel and took a few steps along the footpath towards the canal. With enough distance between them and the building, Gladys gave the command to begin playing. "Play, Mavis!" she screamed.

The music floated from the chapel door, and for a moment, Gladys was back in nineteen-seventy-two, listening to what was to be her favourite song, for the first time. Note after perfect note came one after the other, and Gladys looked at Ethel. "Can you do better?" she said.

"I think Mavis and I are very close in our playing styles," said Ethel. "I'm not sure there'll be much of a difference."

"Humbleness. I like it," said Gladys. "Now get yourself into the chapel and tell Mavis to step outside. It's your turn to impress me. Keep playing *Rocket Man* until I come and tell you to stop, I want to know if I can hear it from the boat. Don't you let me down, Ethel."

Ethel hurried up the pathway, and Willow kicked a stone. "You're taking this very seriously, Granny," she said. "You're coming across as mean."

"Mean breeds obedience," said Gladys. "I want to get the best I can out of them. There's no room for sentimentality in the music business."

A MEETING OF MINDS

"Your picking an organist for your wedding," said Penny. "Not signing an artist to a record label."

Before Gladys could explain that Penny would never amount to anything with *that* attitude, Mavis scurried through the chapel door and made her way towards them. "How did I do? I hope you enjoyed it. The organ made it easier, of course. It really is lovely. I don't think Ethel will have a chance, she seems nervous, and that... *suit* she's wearing really doesn't belong in a chapel. It'll put her off her chords."

Before Mavis could reach them, Ethel began playing, and a smile spread across Gladys's face. That was how *Rocket Man* should be played — with the same enthusiasm Elton had put into writing it. If Mavis had been good, Ethel was proving to be excellent.

Gladys didn't think twice, she waited until Mavis had joined them, took another look at the blue rinse perm, and made her decision. "I think you should go home, Mavis," she said. "You might have the clothes and the... *hair*, but you don't have the dexterous fingers of Ethel, or her ironic dress sense. Asking you to come today was a mistake. I'll reimburse you for your time, and the petrol you used to drive here, but for you, Mavis Buttersworth, the dream is over."

"Really?" said Mavis.

"*Really?*" echoed Penny.

"Granny," said Willow. "That's awful of you."

Mavis appeared to grow an inch in height as she stared at Gladys, an angry glare harshening her face. She took a deep breath, and seemed to get her temper under control. "Have it your way, Gladys. I'm sure Ethel will do a wonderful job, but don't blame me if things don't go to plan, karma has a wonderful way of redressing the balance."

Ethel hit the second verse hard, and Gladys smiled as the music echoed through the valley. "Karma is the last thing that worries me," she said. "I'm more worried about being hit by a meteorite, than I am by superstitious nonsense."

Mavis gave Gladys another firm stare, and turned her face away as Penny approached her with an apologetic expression on her face. "Don't worry, Penelope," she said. "I don't need comforting. My cat is waiting at home for me, that's all the comfort I need."

Gladys felt a twinge of guilt. She knew she could be nasty, but she couldn't be seen to back down either. Sometimes, keeping up appearances could be a very heavy burden to bear. Without wanting to hurt Mavis any further, she turned her back and headed down the path towards the boat. "Come on, girls. Let's find out if we can hear the music from the canal."

Gladys heard Mavis shooing off another attempt from one of her granddaughters to console her, and was pleased when Penny and Willow caught up with her.

"What's got into you, Granny?" said Penny. "That poor woman had hers in her eyes."

"You humiliated her," said Willow.

Gladys stopped walking when they reached the pier. "Okay. I admit it," she said. "I went too far. I often do. I can't help it. I'll be sure to work on it in the future, but come on — you saw her nasty streak rearing its head when Ethel walked into the chapel. She went out of her way to put her down. She's just as mean as I'm accused of being."

"Well I feel awful for her," said Penny. "The poor old —"

Penny couldn't finish her sentence. Gladys pushed past her, rushing back along the pathway. "No, no, no, no, no!" she shouted. "That won't do! What on earth is Ethel playing at? It sounds like she's scalding a cat!"

Penny and Willow joined her, running along the path as the antagonised sound of one continuous high-pitched note echoed through the trees.

Gladys had never understood what people meant when they said their teeth were standing on edge, but as she rushed through the chapel doorway, her hands over her ears, she knew precisely what they were describing. Her teeth vibrated, and her jaw muscles clenched in protest at the siren sound which blasted from the organ. Her head felt violated, and she was beginning to think she'd be forced to run after Mavis and beg her forgiveness if Ethel thought it acceptable to add her own twisted interpretation to a classic Elton song.

She stopped in her tracks. Something was wrong. Gladys had never pretended to have the skills of a detective, but she could see that *something* was amiss. Whether it was the way that Ethel's upper body had collapsed onto the keyboard — her bottom still on the stool, or whether it was the ribbon of blood which ran from the nape of her neck and down her shiny jacket — Gladys wasn't sure — but she did know that her senses were in overdrive., and she was beginning to lose control.

Not now, Gladys, *not now, Gladys*, she repeated in her head — the mantra she used when she knew she was shutting down. Gladys hated the condition she had which caused her to look weak in certain stressful situations. The girls were used to it — they'd seen Gladys shut down before, but it made it no less shameful, and Gladys fought hard to remain in control.

Penny rushed past her, and Willow followed close behind, both girls stopping behind Ethel, their faces ashen. Penny touched Ethel's neck with two fingers, and Willow flicked switches and turned knobs, trying to silence the organ. Finally, and to Gladys's relief, she silenced the noise with a spell. Sometimes Gladys wondered if the girls forgot they were witches.

"She's dead," said Penny, panic rising in her voice. "Somebody's killed her!"

Willow's phone was in her hand. "I'll call the police!"

A distant screeching of tyres and the roar of an engine were the last sounds Gladys heard before her body finally shut down, and the last murky thought she managed was that Mavis was a murderer, as well as being a mediocre organist. *Just how bad could one woman be?*

"GLADYS! GLADYS!"

The voice was distant, but the hand on her forehead was too close. "Get off me!" she said, slapping at the invading digits.

She opened her eyes. The first thought that traversed her mind was that she'd died and gone to hell, but she quickly realised that the fiery red hair did not belong to a demon, loyal to Beelzebub himself, but to Barney Dobkins — Penny's boyfriend and local law enforcement charlatan. Had his breath not been so putrid, Gladys may have come to the latter conclusion first, but anybody who thought it acceptable to breath onion fumes over her face from so far within her personal space, was as close to a demon as she could imagine.

Gladys was on her knees, but that neither worried or surprised her. It was her body's position of choice when she had one of her episodes, and she'd become accustomed to applying Savlon ointment to carpet burns over the years. What *did* concern her, were the words she may have said whilst out of the loop. She'd said some very embarrassing things in the past while her body dealt with an overload of shock, the most cringeworthy being when she regained consciousness on the floor of the *Covenhill Delicatessen and Coffee Shop.* She'd been surrounded by concerned customers, who later told her she'd been clutching a Spanish chipolata, and screaming obscenities about what Farmer Bill, may, or may not have had, in the trouser department.

She'd never worked out what had set the incident off, but she did remember being very anxious about how to correctly pronounce *grande* as she ordered a hot beverage.

Barney moved his face closer to hers. "Are you okay, Gladys?" he said, the radio on his jacket spewing static and excited voices. "You had one of your turns, but you're okay now."

Gladys spoke in hushed tones. "Did I say anything? While I was on the floor?"

Barney shone his flashlight in Gladys's eyes, making her wince. "Something about a monkey… and a coconut… I think. I couldn't really hear you with all the commotion going on in here."

Gladys blinked and gazed around the chapel. It came flooding back in an instant, and she looked away as her eyes rested on the body still hunched over the organ, with two paramedics standing next to it, unable to do any good. She stood up quickly when she saw her granddaughters, accepting Barney's offer of a helping hand. "Why are they questioning the girls?" she said.

Penny and Willow stood together in a corner, casting concerned looks in Gladys's direction over the shoulders of the two policemen who were interrogating them.

"Somebody was murdered," said Barney, looking at Gladys as if she hadn't yet fully regained her faculties. "*Of course* we're going to question them, and you too. Although I know you haven't done anything. It's procedure."

"It was Mavis," said Gladys. "Go and arrest her, and get that poor woman's body out of here. I'm getting married in this chapel in four days time."

"The body will be gone soon enough," said Barney. "But I'm afraid you won't be getting married here. At least not until we've sure we know who murdered Ethel. This building is a homicide investigation scene now, Gladys, and I'm the Sergeant in charge of keeping the scene forensically intact. I'm afraid the chapel is off limits."

Gladys stumbled, pushing Barney's hand away as he tried to steady her. "Not getting married… homicide… scene… investigation," she gasped. "Not on my nelly! I've been without a husband to control for too many years, young man, and if you think a bothersome murder is going to stop me getting married, then you don't know which way is up and which way is down!"

"Granny, are you okay?" said Penny, pushing past the two policemen. "Why are you shouting?"

"Your beau here tells me I won't be getting married on Saturday. That's why I'm shouting."

A tall man dressed in a dark suit looked up, sliding his notebook into his jacket pocket. "What's all the noise about?" he said. "This is a murder scene, not a football match! A good woman has been murdered!"

Gladys wondered how long he'd been a policeman. He looked to be well into his seventies, but he had the inquisitive spark of a much younger man in his narrowed eyes.

"And who the dickens are you?" said Gladys. "This is my chapel. I own it. I'd ask you to show a modicum of respect while you're on my premises."

He fixed Gladys with a stern scowl that made her sigh. If he thought his practised facial expressions would scare her, he didn't know *who* he was dealing with. "I'm Detective Inspector Jameson," he said, "and I'd ask you to control yourself. I'll be needing to speak to you shortly, after all, there's a dead body in a chapel in the middle of nowhere, and you three people were the only ones here when the body was discovered. You seem rather angry, too… do you often have problems controlling your temper?"

Gladys's belly burned with rage. Was *Inspector Grumpy* accusing her of something? A familiar tingle ran the length of her arms, and she knew the shocked looks she was on the receiving end of, were because sparks were flowing from her fingers.

"Granny, no!" yelled Willow.

Too late. Gladys had cast her spell. A shockwave spread through the air, and silence filled the chapel. Time stood still — or seemed to. It was a simple spell that every witch should learn, and the people in the room would come to no harm when Gladys freed them from the hex.

Gladys took a seat on the end of a dirty pew and gathered her thoughts. She'd need to free Penny and Willow from the spell first, and when she'd finished explaining to the girls that they were going to help *her* solve the murder, and they'd willingly agreed to participate, Gladys would release the police officers and paramedics, hexing them with another charm, the details of which she hadn't quite thought through just yet.

Nobody was going to stop Gladys weaver getting married on Saturday. She'd been waiting too long.

CHAPTER SIX

"You cast a spell on us!" said Willow. "Your own grandchildren! Your very own flesh and blood!"

"And Barney," said Penny. "You know he's on your side. He watched you being burned alive in The Haven for goddess's sake, you should have showed him some respect!"

"Burned to death," corrected Gladys. "And I released you two first, didn't I? Anyway, whatever I think of Barney is beside the point. He's still a fed."

"He's a *policeman* who's on *your* side," said Penny. "He was worried sick when he found you shut down on the chapel floor, he ran to you before he even looked at the body!"

"What's your plan?" said Willow, studying the

magically frozen face of the inspector, concerned lines still deeply etched beneath his staring eyes. "This guy doesn't look like he'll take any nonsense. I don't want to be here when you lift the hex."

Gladys pointed at Ethel. "My plan is to prove that Mavis murdered Ethel, find a new organist, and get on with my wedding planning."

"A woman's dead, Granny," said Penny, trying not to look at Ethel's body. "And you're worried about your wedding?"

"Call me old fashioned," said Gladys, "but the dead are the dead. I'll pay my respects to Ethel in my own way. I'll solve her murder and then get on with loving the living. That's what she would have wanted."

"How do you know what she wanted?" said Willow. "You hardly knew her."

Gladys studied the dead body. "Anybody who wears a shell-suit in twenty-seventeen *has* to be a free spirit, and free spirited people are kind people. I'm sure Ethel would want Charleston's love for me to be publicly acknowledged. She wouldn't want her murder to ruin other lives, or my wedding day." She paused for a moment. "At least that's how I know I'd feel. If it was me who'd been murdered mid Elton

A MEETING OF MINDS

John, I'd want everyone else to carry on with their lives."

"What about this little mess?" said Willow, making a sweeping gesture with her arm. "You've got a chapel full of frozen policemen who came here to solve a murder. They're hardly just going to walk out of the door like nothing's happened when you lift the spell."

Gladys had already decided how she was going to deal with that problem. A simple mind cleansing spell would suffice. "I'm going to wipe their minds," she said. "Just of *this* little incident. They'll still remember what they had for breakfast and who they're married to, but they're going to leave the chapel and head back to work with no knowledge of what's gone on here."

"But I phoned the police," said Willow. "And they brought an ambulance with them. The crime will be recorded on the system!"

Gladys thought for a moment. It was about time she earned the reputation of being known as the most powerful witch in the Weaver family. She had begun to think that the rest of her family only allowed her to use the title through misguided sympathy and pity. Well, Gladys hadn't got where she was in life by being a bargain basement witch. She deserved respect. "I've learned a trick or two over the years," she said. "And one of them is how to use an EMP."

"An extremely magical pulse," said Willow. "That would work. Wickford is only a small town, you could easily wipe the memories of everyone involved, and remove the evidence from their computers and phones!"

"You can't be thinking this is a good idea, Willow," said Penny. "What about Barney? I don't want Granny interfering with his thoughts."

"I won't cast any spells on Barney," said Gladys. Although she was more than wiling to if he proved to be a problem. "We'll need his help, and when it's over, and we've banged Mavis to rights, he can take credit for he whole thing. He's got his eye on becoming a detective, hasn't he, Penny? Imagine if Barney solved a crime single handedly. He'd be a hero and get a promotion in no time at all. If he cooperates with me, he'll be out of that uniform in no time. Out of those trousers, darling."

Gladys saw the brief flash of realisation in Penny's eyes as she looked Barney up and down. Everyone knew Barney was too tall to pull off the uniform he wore, especially his girlfriend. Penny frowned. "I don't know…"

Gladys knew she had it in the bag. "Imagine that!

A MEETING OF MINDS

No more trousers which are too short for him. He'll be able to wear his own suits to work when he's a detective, he won't need to rely on the police uniform store-man to make him look like a law enforcement clown."

"I suppose the damage is already done," said Penny, her eyes on the bright white of Barney's exposed socks. "You've already used magic. We may as well see it through. Let me speak to Barney first though. He'll listen to me."

"Fair enough," said Gladys. "Now stand back while I release him. Ginger folk tend to have very short fuses. Does he have a taser?"

"No!" said Penny. "He's a brave unarmed policeman, and he does *not* have a bad temper — as you know. Just release him from your spell please. He's dribbled all over his shirt."

BARNEY AND PENNY stood together in the corner, speaking in loud whispers. Gladys knew the policeman was going to come around to her way of thinking soon enough, despite his wild hand gestures and the beads of sweat dripping from his brow. Penny had the man twisted around her finger, just as it should be in any healthy relationship, and Gladys could see he was quickly weakening.

Willow had conjured a sheet into existence, much to Gladys's delight — maybe the girl *had* been practising her magic as she claimed. With Ethel's body hidden by the sheet, Gladys and Willow sat side by side on a pew and waited for Penny to wear her boyfriend down.

After another full minute of frantic discussions in the corner, Penny turned to face them. "Barney wants to know if you've lost control of your senses."

"Tell him to ask me himself," said Gladys. "There's no need for that sort of childish behaviour. He's a grown man."

"You put a spell on policemen!" snapped Barney. "You've magically assaulted police officers! I'm not being childish!"

"Anybody who has to say their not being childish, normally is being childish. Now pull up your big boy shorts, Barney Dobkins. We've got a murder to solve," said Gladys. "And the longer we take doing it, the harder it will be for you to explain it away. I've cast a stasis spell on Ethel's body, so it will be perfectly preserved. When we solve the murder we'll say we just discovered her, and you can take all the glory for solving it within hours. I know Ethel lives alone, but it won't take forever for somebody to miss her. Time is of the essence!"

Barney gulped. "I'll be lying though. I don't like lying."

Gladys gasped. "There's a dead woman propped up at an organ, Barney, and all you can worry about is your moral integrity? I thought better of you, young man. Now, are with us or against us?"

"With you," muttered Barney, looking at his feet.

"Louder," said Gladys. "And with more enthusiasm please."

He sighed. "With you. I'm with you okay!" Barney looked around the room. "But what about all these people?"

"We discussed that while you were… otherwise occupied," said Granny. "I'm going to cast an extremely magical pulse which will wipe all the evidence of this despicable situation from people's minds, and any electronic devices it may be recorded on. It will be as if it never happened. Only us four and the murderer — my money's on Mavis — will be aware anything happened here today."

"Won't it wipe the memory of the murderer?" said Barney. "Whoever did it was here too. They know what happened. You might make them forget they did it."

Did he really think she was that stupid? Did he *really* think the woman who had once used magic to give Wickford an Indian summer while the rest of Britain was freezing, would make such an elementary error? "Who's the powerful witch, Barney?" said Gladys. "Me or you?"

"Urm… you?"

"Correctamundo. So trust me," said Gladys. "Now. Everybody stand still. When I cast the spell, these people are going to wake up, look a little confused, and go about their day. Don't speak to them or touch them, just let them leave the chapel, okay?"

With everyone in agreement, Gladys rallied her strength, drawing magic from the deepest part of her soul and gathering it in her chest. Her blood pumped quickly, and her ears rang as she lifted her hands. She spoke slowly, and prepared to release the ball of energy which throbbed against her ribs. "Three. Two. One."

Static bubbled in the air, and a shock wave spread from Gladys, moving at speed. Hair on heads was ruffled in the breeze, and birds squawked outside, panicked by the sudden change in air pressure.

Within a few short seconds the spell was cast, and people began moaning as they woke up, gazing around the chapel in confusion. Inspector Jameson looked at his watch, and one of the paramedics took her partners pulse before shaking her head and picking up her bag. "Come on," she said to her partner. "Let's pick up a sandwich on the way back to the hospital. I'm starving."

Inspector Jameson gave the room a cursory glance, and Gladys was pleased to see him tear out the page of notes he'd gathered in his book, and toss the crumpled ball of paper at his feet.

One by one, people filed from the chapel, not speaking to one another, and rubbing their heads. Gladys followed them from the chapel, making sure they were all heading up the track towards the road where their vehicles would be parked. When she was sure her spell had been imbued with the adequate potency she went back inside.

Barney had removed the sheet from Ethel and was examining her body, and Penny had picked up the Inspector's notebook page. Gladys was happy to see they were using their initiatives, she'd not been looking forward to having to crack the whip. People worked better when not under duress, and she needed a strong team if she was to be married in a few days time.

"I'm no pathologist," said Barney. "But it looks like she was stabbed in the back of the neck… with some sort of knife. I assume her death was instant because her fingers are still in position on the keys."

"Rocket Man," said Gladys.

"Thanks," said Barney.

"No," said Gladys. "She was *playing* Rocket Man by Elton John when she died. At least the last sound she heard was a beautiful one."

"Listen," said Penny, reading from the sheet of notebook paper.

"The victim is Ethel Boyd. Could her murder be linked to the incident in 1987? Most probably. Or could it be something to do with the crazy old woman — Gladys Weaver? She has the eyes of a criminal."

Gladys felt the hurt deep in her heart, but it was quickly replaced by anger. Eyes of a criminal? How dare he! She had the eyes of a Hollywood starlet. Stupid flat footed copper. "Never mind all that," said Gladys. "We should go straight to Mavis's house. She's our man — I mean woman. You mark my words." She looked at Barney. "I assume you have a police car parked on the road?"

He nodded. "Yes, but I can't go galavanting about town questioning people. I'll be needed back at the station, people will wonder where I've gone. I don't want to arouse suspicions I've put myself in enough potential trouble as it is."

"Maybe that's for the best," said Gladys. "You should stay out of the way for now. Let us vigilantes get to work. You can take us to my cottage. My Range Rover is still there. Charleston won't let me take it to The Haven. He says I'd ruin the peace. I'll drive us to Mavis's house and Penny will phone you when Mavis has admitted she committed murder, Barney. This whole thing should be wrapped up by tea-time, and you'll be a detective by next week!"

"What about my boat?" said Penny.

"We'll come back for it later, darling" said Gladys. "Don't fret. There's more important things to concern ourselves with. Good grief."

"What if somebody else discovers Ethel's body while we're not here," said Willow.

"Thank you, Willow" said Gladys, Peering at penny over her spectacles. "A *sensible* question at last. That's a very good point, Willow, but a problem which is easily solved. I'll put a spell over the whole of this area, including Penny's boat. It will make people turn away before they get close. They won't know why, but they'll simply turn around and go the other way. Ethel won't be discovered until we want her to be." Gladys peered around the chapel. "Any more questions? Or can we go and visit a certain Mavis Buttersworth? By tonight I want her to be more concerned about becoming somebody's blue-rinse bitch in the big house, than murdering defenceless women as they attempt to impress me with beautiful chord progressions."

CHAPTER SEVEN

Mavis Buttersworth's house irked Gladys, and in her opinion, was just the sort of place a person with murderous tendencies would choose to live. The long lane, potholed and narrow, was easy for her top of the range, highly sought after and envied Range Rover to navigate, but she imagined nobody would take the road unless there was a very good reason for their journey. It was the perfect place for Mavis to remain hidden from the rest of law-abiding society as she planned her next heinous crime.

"Honeysuckle cottage," said Willow, reading the name on the open gate. "It's a beautiful spot."

Gladys gunned the engine, spewing gravel from beneath the chunky tyres. "Beautiful, or sinister?"

"Beautiful," said Penny.

Why the girls deemed it necessary to agree with one another all the time was infuriating. Gladys bit her bottom lip as she brought the vehicle to a halt outside the cottage. "Beauty is in the eye of the beholder. You girls don't see what I see," she said. "You see the flowers and the pretentious ornamental pond. I see a lair for a jealous woman, driven to murder by her inability to match her better on the organ keyboard."

"She's got a dove loft!" said Willow. "How lovely!"

Gladys felt a twinge of pity for the girls. It must be hard to go through life with such a simple and foolish outlook. She regretted bringing the girls with her. It seemed they weren't suited to police work in the slightest. *Never-mind.* Gladys was confident in her own abilities — she'd bring Mavis down alone. "Forget the dove loft," she said, killing the engine and opening her door. "Because those doves won't be around for much longer anyway. When Mavis is doing porridge they'll soon bugger off when they realise nobody's coming to feed them. Doves are like cats. They're selfish and they're nomads. They'll be in another loft before you can say—"

"What a glorious beast!"

This was awkward. Nobody had ever complimented Gladys on her vehicle before. She assumed it was because of jealousy and a needy longing to possess what they would never own. Mavis, on the other hand, seemed genuinely thrilled to have such a feat of magnificent engineering parked outside her home. Gladys knew she had to accuse the woman of murder, but doing it before she'd finished having her ego massaged, was not something Gladys was prepared to do. "Thank you!" she said. "It's a wonderful vehicle. Fast, practical, and a real head-turner. It's not bad on fuel either, which was a finacially pleasant surprise."

"I bet it gets all the boys!' said Mavis, with a wink, hurrying down her garden path, her straw-hat askew, and a pair of gardening secateurs in one hand. "I heard it all the way from the back garden! I bet the men love it!"

"I wouldn't know!" giggled Gladys, returning the wink with a twisting of her head. She hoped the simple head movement placed adequate emphasis on the subsequent wink, because Gladys *certainly* knew what Mavis was talking about. She'd lost count of the number of times men had pulled alongside her at red lights, laughing and pointing at her, engaging in the silly flirtatious teasing that men seemed to enjoy so much. "I'm getting married on Saturday, silly! Men are of no interest to me!" A thought leapt into Gladys's mind. *Fate.* It had to be. "Oh, that reminds me," she gushed. "I'm going to need an organist, are you free on—"

"Granny!" said Willow, under her breath. "Are you forgetting something? Take a deep breath and remember why we're here."

"Come on, Willow," whispered Gladys, watching Mavis run an appreciative hand over the smooth black lines of the car. "Does she look like a murderer to you? She looks like a woman with fine taste to me. I've even warmed to her hair-do. I might ask her where she had it done." Gladys lowered her voice even further. "Or would that be too rude?"

"Did you come here to ask me to be your organist, Gladys?" said Mavis, kicking a tyre. "Because I'd love to be! Did Ethel let you down? Is that why you've come? I heard that terrible racket she was making as I walked away from the chapel. It sounded like she was scalding a cat, not practising for the most important day of your life."

"That's just what I thought!" said Gladys. "Scalding a cat! I like you, Mavis. We've a lot in common."

Penny sighed. "Granny," she said. "I'd like to *speak* to Mavis."

Gladys hated it when people put emphasis on a word, and she was *sure* that she wasn't guilty of the same abuse of the English language. "Oh you would, *would* you?" Two could play at that game.

Penny said something under her breath, and a sizzle in the air next to her told her Gladys that her granddaughter was about to cast a spell. "Oh! *Speak*," she said. "I see. Good idea, darling."

Mavis was too busy admiring the storage space the boot of the Range Rover had to offer, to see the dancing lights at Penny's fingertips, but as the spell hit her she made a strangled groan and stood up straight, her eyes devoid of any emotion and her fingers losing their grip on the gardening implement.

"What spell was that?" said Willow, waving her hand in front of Mavis's unblinking eyes.

"A truth spell with a little amnesia thrown in," said Penny. "When she wakes up she won't remember anything, but she'll answer any question truthfully."

"Well done!" said Gladys. It was wonderful to see her granddaughters following in her magical footsteps, and Gladys was happy to give the floor to Penny. "Ask away, sweetheart," she said. "It's your spell. Just make sure you ask the right questions."

Penny stared into Mavis's eyes. "Do you know Ethel Boyd is dead, Mavis?"

"No," Mavis said.

Penny licked her lips. "Did you kill Ethel Boyd?"

Gladys watched carefully. It was impossible to lie whilst under the influence of a truth spell. The answer to Penny's first question didn't necessarily mean that Mavis was innocent. She may have stabbed Ethel and left the chapel before checking to see if her victim had succumbed to her injuries.

Mavis answered quickly and with conviction. "No. I didn't kill Ethel Boyd."

Gladys allowed herself a smile. Then frowned. Yes, she was now free to use Mavis as her organist, but now it had been proved Mavis was innocent, the murder had become harder to solve. If Gladys knew one thing about herself, though, it was that she always achieved what she put her mind to, and she was adamant that she was getting married on Saturday. *She'd find the real killer in time.*

Penny continued with her questions. "Do you know who might have killed Ethel, or why they might have killed her?"

"No. Ethel keeps herself to herself. I don't know who would do such a thing."

"Did you see anybody near the chapel, Mavis? When you walked back to your car?" asked Penny. "Or hear anything suspicious?"

"I heard a rustle in the bushes, but when I looked, it was a dog. A little white terrier. I didn't stay to stroke it though, it's owner was probably nearby, and that horrendous musical note that Ethel was playing was hurting my ears. That organ was really loud — and very well made, almost like it had been made by the hands of a master tradesman. I'm surprised I heard the dog over the noise, but I've always had good ears. And feet."

"You're losing her, Penny,' said Gladys. "She's going off on tangents. Let me ask her a question before she snaps out of it."

"Go ahead," said Penny, casting a flurry of green sparks over Mavis's straw-hat. "That should hold her for a little while more, but she's strong willed, she won't stay under for long."

Gladys imagined what her favourite TV detective would ask Mavis. Columbo always got his man, and *he* had a glass eye. With her glasses giving her perfect vision, Gladys was certain she could be just as effective as the detective. If not twice as good. "Mavis," she said, wondering if one of the thrift shops in town sold weathered brown raincoats. "Has Ethel said anything strange recently, or has she been doing anything out of character? Has she been sad, happy, angry… or even scared?"

Mavis groaned. "I only see Ethel at the bowling club. We're not great friends, but I did hear her telling the clique she's in that she was feeling better since visiting that new hypnotherapist in town. You know, the chubby gay one. The one with lovely dress sense." She blinked. "My head hurts. Am I real?"

Gladys swelled with pride. Hearing her son spoken about in such beautiful terms was music to her ears. "She's snapping out of it," she said. "Just carry on as if nothing's happened."

Willow stepped forward and bent over to pick up Mavis's secateurs. "Here you are, Mavis," she said handing them to the confused woman. "You dropped these."

"Did I?" said Mavis. "My, my, this sun is strong, isn't it? I went a little dizzy just then, I think I need a cup of tea. Would anyone else like one?"

"No thank you," said Gladys. "We've got important work to do, but Mavis, I have a request to ask of you. Would you be the organist at my wedding on Saturday?"

"Yes!" said Mavis instantly. "Yes! I will be your organist, Gladys! Oh how lovely! I hope Ethel isn't too upset, have you told her yet, Gladys?"

Gladys searched deep inside herself for the appropriate answer. Images of Columbo and Sherlock

Holmes entwined in her mind's eye, and she gathered herself as she delivered her sarcastic, yet witty, punchline. "Ethel won't mind, Mavis, and anyway, compared to you, she's a like a corpse playing the organ."

"THAT WAS a disgusting thing to say, Granny," said Willow. "Really disgusting. You don't joke about dead people. It's wrong."

"Lighten up," said Gladys. "It made Mavis laugh, didn't it?"

"Mavis didn't know Ethel *is* a corpse, Granny," said Penny. "She thought you were complimenting her. I don't think she'd have laughed if she *had* known."

Gladys brought the Range Rover to a stop behind the police car parked on the side of the road. She was happy to be back at the chapel — she'd had to put up with criticism of her witty one-liner for the whole of the journey. She'd only been trying to lighten the mood. "Good, Barney's here already," she said.

"Of course he's here," said Penny. "You phoned him and told him we'd hit a complication in the case, and if he didn't get here *pronto*, the whole thing might fall apart and he would end up in prison for attempting to cover up a murder. You told him that feds don't get it easy in the big-house, and a pretty boy like him wouldn't last a night, let alone until breakfast time."

Had Penny really needed to memorise every word she'd said to Barney? It seemed a little show-offy and very unnecessary. Penelope needed to learn to prioritise if she was to be a successful amateur sleuth. Besides, that wasn't *all* Gladys had said. She'd told Barney about the dog and Ethel's visits to her son's hypnotherapist business too. "A little fire lit under him is what he needs," said Gladys. "We're going to need to use some good old fashioned police work from hereon in, and Barney's going to have to be on top of his game. I was just trying to install some urgency in him."

"Well, mission accomplished," said Willow. "Judging by the skid marks behind his car, he wasn't wasting any time when he got here."

THE WALK to the chapel took them less than five minutes, and Gladys crossed herself before she entered the building.

"You're not religious, Granny," said Willow. "You're a witch. You've got your immortality sorted out in The Haven, and anyway, you said your wedding was going to be secular."

"Maybe Ethel was, dear," said Gladys. "It was for her, and this *was* a place of worship at one time, after all. I'm being respectful."

Barney was busy at work when they entered, and he looked up, his face red and his eyes panicked. "I've had a good look around," he said, getting straight to the point, which impressed Gladys. She was a fan of urgency. "I can't find any footprints leading into the trees or any sign of a dog. I can't find anything that the murderer might have dropped, and thanks to you, Gladys, I can't ask the fingerprinting department to come and check the place over."

"Calm your horses, big-boy," said Gladys. "Take a chill-pill." She looked at Penny. "Was that right?"

Penny nodded. "Yes. Chill-pill."

"What do you mean — chill?" said Barney. "How can I chill? There's a dead body in this chapel, and I'm a policeman. I'm in a lot of trouble if my involvement in all… *this*, ever gets out."

"Calm down. What about Ethel's body?" said Gladys. "Are there any clues on it?"

Barney tugged a pair of blue plastic gloves from

his hands and put them in his pocket. "I've had a good look at her. It looks like it happened very quickly, and apart from an old wound on her head and the stab wound in the back of her neck, there's nothing more to see without a forensic examination."

"Old wound?" said Penny.

Barney nodded and wiped sweat from his forehead. "An old scar, a big one on the top of her head. It looks like she was lucky to have survived it."

"What about the stab wound?" said Willow. "Can you tell what sort of knife was used?"

"I don't know," said Barney. "A small one, certainly not a hunting knife — the wound is too small."

"What about that note the detective had written?" said Penny. "I gave it to you. Did you check it out?"

Barney gave an exasperated sigh. "Of course I did. That's the first thing I did when I got back to the station, but I can't find any mention of Ethel Boyd in the system, and definitely not from nineteen-eighty-seven."

"So why did the detective write it down?" said Willow.

"He's been in the force for nearly forty years," said Barney. "He's an old hat. He probably remembered something. Something that's not in the system.

That's what they did back then. They trusted their memories rather than a computer system."

"So what next?" said Willow. "What do we do now? We've got nothing to go on."

"I suggest you undo all this magic," said Barney. "We report the murder, and you find somewhere else to get married, Gladys."

"Oh, Barney," said Gladys. "That's not going to happen, sweetheart. I came here from The Haven to make the final arrangements for my wedding, and I am not going back there to tell my betrothed that I failed at such a simple task. He already thinks disaster follows me everywhere I go, and I won't have him proved right. *We're* going to solve this little problem, and we're going to do it quickly."

Barney's eyes lit up. "Why didn't we think of it sooner!" he said. "Of course! It's so simple! Probably."

"What?" said Penny. "What's simple?"

Barney ignored Penny, and turned his excited face to Gladys. "Gladys, I've seen the sort of magic you're capable of! Surely you can cast a spell like the ones I've seen on the telly, you know, replay the whole scene in front of us! It'll be like watching a film of the murder, but with ghostly figures as people. All the magic people on TV shows and films do it!"

The realisation came to Gladys so hard it made her gasp. Finally, after all those long years, she understood why the teachers at her school had been so frustrated when she hadn't been able to grasp simple concepts. It was enraging, Gladys realised. *The teachers had been enraged with her, just as she was with Barney.*

Gladys had repeatedly asked stupid questions in school, like the one Barney had just asked — no wonder she'd been rapped on the hand with a wooden ruler so frequently — just looking at Barney's enquiring face made her want to clip him around the ear.

"Well?" said Barney. "Can you do it?"

Gladys opened her mouth to speak, but had second thoughts. Maybe it would be therapeutic to her if she spoke to Barney in the way she'd have *liked* the teachers to have spoken to her. Maybe she'd have responded better to kindness, than she had a length of hard wood across the knuckles.

She twisted her face into the kindly expression she saved for anybody who was about to be involved in the preparation of food that she'd ordered — she'd heard too many horror stories about spit being found in soup, to risk upsetting a waitress or a chef. "Oh, Barney," she said gently. "You poor simple child. You lovely idiot. Of course I can't do what you ask."

"There's no need for that," said Barney. "I'm not stupid."

Gladys gave up on kindness. If Barney couldn't recognise his own inadequacies, then Gladys wasn't about to sugarcoat them for him. "You're a blathering simpleton, Barney Dobkins," she said. "Do I look like a witch, or a time traveller? I'll give you a clue… I'm *not* a time traveller, I'm a witch. I can't turn back time like something you saw on the television. Goddess give me strength!"

"Granny!" said Penny. "Don't speak to him like that! He doesn't know what you can and can't do!"

Gladys began pacing. "I'm going to have to take on the role of lead-investigator, it seems. Barney, are you still on side, despite the things I just said to you?"

"Yes," muttered Barney. "I suppose."

Gladys nodded. "Good. We need you, and Ethel needs you. I want you to go back to the police station and try and keep trying to find out what happened in nineteen-eighty-seven, okay? If inspector Jameson thought it was relevant then maybe it is. The rest of us will go and speak to my son, and find out what Ethel was seeing him about. Everyone clear?"

"I'll meet you in town," said Penny. "I'll take the

boat back to the mooring. Willow and I live on it, and I'm not sleeping on a part of the canal next to a chapel with a dead body in it."

"You do that," said Gladys. "I respect your reasoning. Willow and I will go and speak to Brian. You can make a bed up for me on the boat, I'm not going back to The Haven until I can tell Charleston that the wedding is going ahead as planned. I'll be living with you for a little while."

Penny seemed pleased to be having her Granny stay onboard the boat, and she even gave Willow a covert look when she thought Gladys couldn't see.

"I'll check on the shop too," said Penny. "Susie offered to look after it while we took you to the chapel. I said we'd only be an hour, I'm surprised she's not phoning me every five minutes."

The Spell Weavers was a nice little magic shop, but Gladys couldn't see for the life of her why the girls continued to run it. Not since Gladys had come into her newfound income stream. She was more than happy to give them both money whenever they wanted it. She supposed the girls liked feeling independent, and Gladys wouldn't take that away from them, although she knew without doubt that capitalism was the root of most of the evil in the world. Apart from luxury car dealerships, of course — they provided a necessary service which fuelled the economy.

Having their journalist friend living in the flat above the shop was turning out to be mutually beneficial. Susie looked after the shop for the girls when she could, and the girls provided Susie with all the incense and crystals the young girl needed to sort out her chakras. Gladys wasn't going to have her murder investigation interrupted by frantic telephone calls from Susie every few minutes, though, and she'd already taken steps to avoid that.

"She probably is ringing every five minutes," said Gladys. "I put a curse on both of your phones, I was fed up of hearing buzzes and bings every few minutes. There's life outside of social media you know. Now, come on, people, we've got work to do."

With everyone dancing to her beautifully orchestrated tune, and the girls checking their phones, Gladys led her team out of the chapel and ensured the building, and Ethel's body, were still protected by magic.

CHAPTER EIGHT

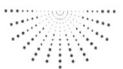

*B*rian was saying goodbye to a client as Willow and Gladys entered his office. Or was it studio? Gladys didn't know, and neither did she care.

"Thank you, Brian," said the stick thin woman as she handed over a wad of notes. "I already feel like I'll never touch another cigarette!" She glanced at Gladys and Willow. "Whatever problems you've come to have solved, I can assure you, Brian will help. He's a miracle worker."

Gladys was in awe of Brian, and she ignored Maggie when she insinuated that it was unethical for Brian to cure people with magic, and charge them for hypnotherapy. Sibling rivalry was an awful thing, and Maggie suffered terribly from it. Gladys couldn't have been prouder of her son, though, and she suspected that people would gladly pay more if they *knew* it was magic that had cured them.

"Mother!" said Brian, as the client left the shop with a parting smile. "Willow! How lovely to see you both. What do you think of the waiting room? I've freshened it up a little since you were last here."

Gladys thought it looked marvellous, and Willow had what Gladys assumed was a look of proud astonishment on her face.

"Who are those handsome girls on the posters?" said Gladys, hooking her arm through her sons. He'd put on weight, she could tell, but he had an excuse — he was a busy man. Maggie, on the other hand, had no excuse whatsoever for being as round as a biscuit barrel, and on Friday nights at least, consisting solely of similar contents.

Brian pointed at the posters in turn. "That's Kylie," he said, "and the gorgeous one next to her is the queen of pop herself."

Gladys squinted. Maybe her glasses weren't working properly. The woman in the poster, with half of her cleavage on show, looked nothing like the queen of pop to her. The cone shaped bra was something the queen of pop wouldn't have been seen dead in. "That's not Cilla Black, is it, darling?" she said. "I don't remember her being that overt with her sexuality. She was always the nice girl next door type."

"It's Madonna, Granny," said Willow.

"Thank goodness for that," said Gladys. "I really didn't like thinking of Cilla looking like that. She was always so wholesome." She squeezed her son's arm. "It looks lovely in here, and you should be proud of yourself."

"Thank you, Mother," said Brian. "Are you ready for your wedding? I can't wait to walk you down the aisle. I've chosen my suit and polished my shoes. It's going to be a lovely day!"

Gladys slid her arm away from Brian. "That's why we're here, sweetie. There's been a problem with the chapel, and if we don't sort it out soon, there might not be a wedding on Saturday."

"Oh no!" said Brian, putting a guarding hand over his chest. "What's happened? Let me guess… a rare species of bat has been found living in the chapel, and it's against the law to move them?"

"Oh gosh, no!" said Gladys. "Nothing that drastic. I'd have no chance of sorting that type of problem out by Saturday… you can't just shoo rare bats away with magic. The poor creatures wouldn't know what to do! No, the problem's not quite in that ball-park."

"Thank Goddess," said Brian. "What is it then?"

Gladys lowered her voice as if the walls had ears. "A woman was murdered in the chapel this morning. Whilst playing *Rocket Man* on the organ. Stabbed in the back of the neck, would you believe? It's all very sad, but I need to find out who did it as quickly as possible. We can mourn at a later date. Perhaps."

"I'm glad you think it's sad, Granny," said Willow, a condescending look in her eyes. "Listening to you would lead people to believe it was simply a minor spanner in the works of your wedding arrangements."

Brian stumbled, and collapsed into one of the big leather seats he'd installed for waiting clients. "Not Ethel?" he said. "Please don't tell me it was Ethel."

"I'm afraid so, son," said Gladys, patting the big man on his head. Brian always had enjoyed physical affection from his mother, so Gladys formed a fist and monkey scrubbed his scalp. "That's why we came here. We found out that she was a client of yours. We need to know why she was seeing you, it could help with finding out who killed her."

Brian pushed his mother's hand away and stood up. "Have you heard of client confidentiality?" he said. "Good heavens!"

"Have you heard of a clip around the ear?" said Gladys. "You're not to big to put over my knee, you know!" She suspected he was. She also suspected he'd fight back, so Gladys hoped she wasn't forced to implement corporal punishment as encouragement to make him sing.

"I could get in trouble!" said Brian. "I could lose my business!"

"Uncle Brian," said Willow. "You use magic and pretend you're a hypnotherapist. You're on quite thin ice already."

"*And* you've chosen your suit and polished your shoes, dear," said Gladys. "If we don't find out who killed Ethel, you'll not be wearing them on Saturday."

"Poor Ethel," said Brian, defeatedly lowering himself into the seat once more. "She worked so hard to make sure she could step inside that chapel again. Magic could only get her so far, the anxiety was so deeply embedded — she did most of the work herself. She was really hoping you'd pick her to play the organ. She needed the money you were offering, and she said it would be like facing her demons."

Gladys and Willow sat down too. Gladys on the seat next to her son's, and Willow on the chaise lounge. "Tell me everything," said Gladys.

Brian sighed. "She came to see me on the day you offered her and another woman the chance to play the organ at your wedding."

"Mavis," said Gladys. "And we've already ruled her out as a jealous murderer. I didn't really think it was her anyway, she's far too nice."

"That's right," said Willow. "You never thought it was Mavis."

Gladys wondered how many times Willow could roll her eyes in one day without causing permanent damage to her sight.

Brian loosened his tie, allowing a shaved roll of fat to bulge over his shirt collar. "Yes, Mavis," he said, with a nod. "Ethel really wanted you to choose her over Mavis, but first she had to drum up the courage to step inside the chapel."

"Why?" said Willow.

"Something happened there," said Brian. "I don't know what it was, she wouldn't tell me. It was a long time ago though, and she kept touching the back of her head when she spoke about it — you need to notice these things when you're in a position of trust like I am. Sometimes the actions of a client speak louder than their words."

"The old head wound," said Willow.

"Nineteen-eighty-seven," said Gladys.

"What?" said Brian.

Gladys filled her son in on the day's events, being

sure to mention that Mavis had loved her car, and that Barney was in her pocket.

Brian listened carefully until Gladys had finished, and then closed his eyes for a moment. "I've always liked the idea of a dove loft," he said, "but not with a nice car on the property. Unless it was garaged of course. Those birds could shit for Britain. You'd be forever washing it, and that's not good for the paintwork."

"Indeed," said Gladys, "they're dirty buggers. Flying rats."

"That's pigeons," noted Brian. "Not doves. Doves are the bird of peace."

Willow leaned forward. "Let me just bring this… conversation back on track," she said, tapping her foot on the floor in the annoying way which Gladys knew showed her impatience with a situation. "So all you can tell us, Uncle Brian, is that something happened to Ethel in the chapel a long time ago. Something that made her anxious about going back there?"

Brian nodded. "Yes," he said. "Oh! And that she needed the money of course. Money is often a reason for murder. That could be relevant."

"Did she say why she needed the money?" said Willow.

"No," said Brian. "She just said her circumstances had changed. She said she'd been used to receiving a payment each month, but it had dried up. I think she was quite poor. She said she could only just afford my fee, but I didn't pry — as long as a client can afford to pay me — I can't afford to care about their financial situation. I need to eat too."

"You have to be like that," said Gladys. "You're running a business, son, not a charity! People will take advantage of you if you let them, and you've got such a lovely big heart — they'd walk all over you."

Willow sighed. She really was a rude young lady — with all the eye rolling and emphasised breathing. "So we're done here?" she said.

"Have some patience, dear," said Gladys. "It's good for your health." She looked at her son. "Is there anything else you can think of, Brian? Anything else she may have said?"

He shook his head. "No. It's such a shame though isn't it? Ethel was a very religious woman. She told me that the chapel had been her rock until the incident which stopped her from going there again. What a terrible thing — to be killed in the place that once gave you so much comfort. It would be like me being murdered in *The Pink Pamper — Men's Hair Salon and Eatery*. What an awful, awful thought."

THE SMELL of cooking greeted Gladys and Willow as they approached *The Water Witch*, and Rosie ran across the grass to greet them, weaving in and out of their legs.

Inside the boat, Susie was helping Penny prepare a lamb stew, and Gladys gave her a kiss on the cheek as she squeezed past her in the narrow galley kitchen. She liked Susie. She was a respectful young lady with good morals and an honest job.

"I hear you cast a spell on the whole of the Wickford police force *and* their computer systems," said Susie. "And you've taken it upon yourself to hide the fact that a woman is dead, just so you can stop a murder investigation from messing up your wedding plans. Have you gone senile? What were you thinking?"

Gladys smiled. She loved Susie's banter. She gave the cheeky girl a playful elbow nudge in her ribs, and laughed as Susie dropped the salt shaker she was holding. "Be sure to throw some over your shoulder," Gladys said. "It's bad luck otherwise."

Susie muttered something under her breath.

"What was that?" said Gladys, certain the girl had

cursed. There was banter, and there was disrespect. Gladys would take none of the latter.

"I said 'I *need* some luck.'"

"Oh," said Gladys. "Well throw a double helping over your shoulder."

"Sit down, Granny," said Penny. "Let's eat. Susie has something to tell you, too. About the incident Inspector Jameson referred to in nineteen-eighty-seven."

With her interest piqued and her belly rumbling, Gladys sat down and reached for a hunk of buttered bread as Penny placed a plate on the table. She hadn't realised how hungry she was, and if she didn't eat before seven o'clock in the evening she wouldn't stay regular, and nobody could be expected to solve a murder without their bowels in tip-top condition. "What can you tell us?" she said, as Susie put the pot of stew in the centre of the table and sat down.

Susie filled a bowl with stew and passed it to Gladys. Gladys raised an eyebrow, but decided to say nothing. Susie wasn't to know that she wasn't the biggest fan of mushrooms being chopped in half. It was lazy — if she couldn't be bothered to chop the mushrooms into easily swallowed cubes, then what must her underwear drawer look like? A tangled mess, most likely.

"Susie looked the incident up on the internet," said Penny.

"If it's not in the police records it's hardly likely to be on the internet… is it?" said Willow.

Susie smiled. "Not anywhere you could find it," she said, "but as a journalist I'm privy to some private forums. One of them is used by a lot of retired journalists with too much time on their hands. Anyway, I posted a question when Penny told me what had happened."

"And?" said Gladys, using her spoon to break a mushroom apart. Maybe Susie would get the message through visual imagery.

"I got a reply," said Susie. "From a man who was a reporter in Wickford until nineteen-eighty-eight, but get this… he was sent to jail…" she smiled, "…for refusing to stop trying to find out what had happened in a *certain* chapel in a *certain* year."

Gladys frowned. "What chapel, and what year? Wait! I bet it was my chapel! And I bet it was nineteen-eighty-seven!" The looks the three girls gave her told her all she needed to know. "I'm right, aren't I? Tell me I'm right!"

"Erm… yes," said Susie. "But I just practically told yo—"

"Bingo!" said Gladys. "I knew I could be a detective. Go on, Susie, what did he tell you?"

She coughed, and Gladys hoped a mushroom was lodged in her wind-pipe. Maybe she'd only learn the hard way.

Susie took a sip of lemon water. "He said that in July of nineteen-Eighty-Seven, he was fishing on the canal, near the chapel. He owned a small rowing boat, and was anchored just off the pier."

"Is that relevant?" said Gladys. "If not, get to the meat and potatoes of the story. Leave out the massive mushrooms."

"Huh?" said Susie. "Erm… anyway, he heard a commotion. Lots of shouting and engine noise. That sort of thing. Of course the chapel was in use in those days, but it was early in the morning, on a Wednesday. There shouldn't have been that many people there."

"Engines?" said Willow. "But cars can't get down to the chapel. There's only a footpath."

"All part of what happened," said Susie. "They filled the road in a week after the incident and turned it into a footpath. The chapel was closed down too. It was privately owned, and was never used again."

"A Cover-up!" said Gladys.

Susie nodded. "The reporter went ashore," she

said. "There was an ambulance and three police cars outside the chapel. Somebody was being put in the ambulance with two medics working on them, and a man was being put in the back of a police car. In handcuffs."

"What had happened?" said Willow.

"That's where it took a turn down conspiracy lane," said Susie. "The reporter was approached by a policeman and told to leave the area immediately or he'd be arrested. He argued, but he could tell the police were serious, so he left, thinking he'd come back later and find out what had happened."

"And?" said Gladys. "Did he go back?"

"That's when it got *really* sinister. That night, three plain-clothed police officers turned up at his house. The policeman who'd turned him away from the chapel must have recognised him."

"What did they want?" said Willow.

"To silence him," said Susie. "They began nicely, by telling him a mystery benefactor was prepared to pay him a sum of money every month if he never mentioned the incident again, but when he refused, they became threatening. They showed him a warrant for his arrest, signed by a judge, and told him that if he ever went near the chapel again, or mentioned the incident to anybody, he'd be arrested and sent to jail.

They told him he'd bypass court and a trial, and be locked away for a long time."

"What did he do?" said Gladys.

"Although it wasn't that long ago," said Susie. "Times were different, and the reporter knew the police could get away with it. He did what they asked, he kept quiet, and nothing was mentioned about the incident. No reports in any newspapers, no talk in town — nothing, it was like it had never happened. He wouldn't accept any money though. He said it would make him complicit in whatever crime had been committed. He said he was convinced that whoever was being put in the back of the ambulance had died, and that the police were covering up a murder. He wanted no part in it."

"An honest man," said Gladys. "But why did he get sent to jail?"

"He became curious again," said Susie. "A year later. He went back to the chapel, but found nothing. No sign that anything had ever happened there. So he started asking questions in Covenhill hospital. It was the biggest hospital in the area and he assumed the person in the ambulance would have been taken there."

"And?" said Gladys.

"Nothing. Nobody knew anything — or they

wouldn't say anything, but two days later he was visited by two more police-officers. They arrested him on a bogus drug dealing charge. The judge believed all the *evidence*, and he went down for two years. When he got out he moved to London and put it all behind him, until a few years later. When he received a mystery phone-call."

Gladys swallowed a piece of lamb. Mushrooms aside, the stew was good, but Susie's story was better. "A call from who?" she said.

"A man who said he'd been a police officer in Wickford at the time of the incident," explained Susie. "The call was quick. The caller told the reporter that the evidence he needed was in storage beneath Wickford police station. A secret file, he said, locked away and not in any official records. The reporter thought about trying to find out more, but prison had been hard on him, he didn't want to go through it again, so he got on with his life. He tried to forget about the whole thing… until he saw my post on the forum today."

"This is getting too serious,' said Penny. "We should reverse all the spells you've cast, Granny, and let the police deal with it. It's out of our league."

Gladys wiped her mouth on a paper towel, happy that she had something more important than the size of mushrooms to ponder over. "Nonsense," she said. "We need that police file, and we need to go to Ethel's house. Brian told Willow and me that Ethel had suddenly become poor when a monthly payment had dried up — didn't that reporter get offered a monthly sum of money to keep his mouth shut? Coincidence? Maybe, but I'd take fate over coincidence on any day of the week. I want to find out more about Ethel, and I want that police file, so somebody get me my evening sherry, I suggest we all have an early night — it's going to be a busy day tomorrow."

CHAPTER NINE

"There are no old files in the basement anymore," said Barney. "They were moved last year when we had the refurb, and lots of them were shredded. The ones that survived are in Covenhill police station, under lock and key, only accessible to detectives investigating cold cases and historical crimes. I don't have security clearance. You've got no chance of finding it... if it even exists at all."

"Are you doubting Susie's source?" said Gladys. "Do you want to find out who murdered Ethel Boyd?"

Barney tried the door. It was locked. "I'm here, aren't I? About to break into a dead woman's home with my girlfriend and her grandmother — *I'd* say I want to find out who murdered her, wouldn't you?"

"Ignore her," said Penny, pushing past Barney.

"She's cranky because an owl kept her awake last night. She's not used to sleeping on the canal."

"Blasted thing," said Gladys. "Hooting at all hours of the night. Anyone would think it was *trying* to disturb my sleep."

Penny touched the door and said a few words. The lock clicked, and she turned the brass knob. "There, it's open," she said.

Gladys wished she had somebody who looked at her with such loving admiration when she used magic. When *she* cast a spell, all she received was complaints and hissy fits, but Barney was staring at Penny as if she'd made herself invisible, not cast a simple lock opening spell.

"Amazing," murmured Barney. "You're an amazing witch, Penny. I'm so proud of you."

"Thank you," said Penny, pushing the door open and blushing.

"Just get inside," said Gladys. "It's secluded here, but we don't want to risk being seen."

Ethel's little house was tucked away from the road, hidden by a tall leylandii hedge that Gladys imagined would be a bitch to keep under control. Norman had once planted three of the trees in their back garden, but Gladys had scorched them to the ground with a fire spell after they had grown too quickly and blocked the view of her daughter's cottage on the hill on the other side of the valley. Gladys's binoculars were powerful, but even they couldn't see what Maggie was up to through an evergreen hedge.

Barney's police car was parked behind the hedge, hidden from the road, and Gladys doubted very much that anyone would bother them. She followed Barney and Penny into the house and closed and locked the door behind her.

"What are we looking for?" said Penny, gazing around the hallway.

Gladys had liked Ethel, but she didn't think much of her taste in decor. The hallway would have benefited from an antique oak telephone stand, instead of the modern flat packed one which stood in a corner, and wooden flooring took the warmth out of a room, in her opinion. "Bank statements,"'said Gladys, staring at a picture.

Describing it as a picture was too kind — it looked as if the artist had painted it while in the cruel grip of a fit. "I want to find out what those monthly payments were, but I'm beginning to think Ethel was more modern than her age let on. I bet she does all that fancy online banking."

Barney handed them both a pair of latex gloves.

"Put these on," he instructed, "and remind me to wipe the door on the way out. We don't want to take more risks than we have to. If we can't find out who killed Ethel, the forensic guys will be all over this place as soon as the murder comes to light."

"Oh, we'll find out,' said Gladys, slipping the gloves over her fingers. "Of that, I have no doubt. Now, take a room each. I'll start upstairs."

Gladys took the steps quickly for a woman of… her age, and dipped into the first bedroom she saw. It was a small room, probably a guest room, and she found nothing of interest in the one piece of furniture which stood against the wall.

The next room was bigger, and was filled with the lived in smell which told Gladys she was standing in a dead woman's bedroom. Photographs dotted the surface of a chest of drawers, and Gladys picked one up, handling it carefully, her gloves protecting the ornate metal frame from smudges and fingerprints.

The photo showed Ethel and another woman standing together on a beach, both of them smiling, and their hair windswept. Ethel had kind eyes, and her friend looked happy to be in her company.

"I *will* find out who killed you, Ethel," said Gladys to the empty room. "And if you *are* watching me from somewhere, you'll know I'm not as cruel as

I make out." A tear warmed her cheek, and she smiled. "It's hard being a strong matriarch to a family of mad witches, Ethel, but rest assured that most of it's for show, and I care deeply about finding your killer. I know you won't be at my wedding in body, but I'm sure you'll be there in spirit, and you will be most welcome. Mavis is a good organ player, but you'd have been my first choice, Ethel. I hope you know that."

"Who are you talking to, Granny?"

Gladys put the picture down and wiped her eyes. "Just an empty room, dear," she said, turning to face her granddaughter. "Have you and Barney found anything?"

"Just this," said Penny, holding out a computer tablet. "There's not much furniture to search downstairs, it seems Ethel was a minimalist. Barney's just tidying away some paperwork we emptied out of a drawer. What about you? Have you found anything?"

Gladys shook her head. "Not yet, but I haven't checked this chest of drawers yet."

"I'll help you," said Penny.

Between them they checked the drawers in less than a minute, and apart from a pair of knickers which Gladys considered to be very risqué for a woman of Ethel's age, there was nothing of interest to be found.

A MEETING OF MINDS

As Penny closed the bottom drawer, the sound of a car engine drew their attention. "Who's that?" said Penny, peering through the window. "It's pulled up outside, next to Barney's car."

Gladys watched as the car door opened. "It's that Inspector Jameson! What in heavens is he doing here?"

"Hide!" shouted Barney from downstairs. "My boss is here! I'll try and cover for us, but I don't know what the hell he's doing here. No one knows we're here apart from Susie and Willow, and no one knows Ethel is dead!"

Susie and Willow had stayed behind — Susie trying to find out more information about the mysterious incident from three decades ago, and Willow accepting an order of crystals and cast iron cauldrons in *The Spell Weavers*. Gladys very much doubted that either of them would have told anybody that Barney and two witches were breaking into a house. Inspector Jameson must have found out by other means.

"Deep breaths, Barney," shouted Gladys, hearing the panic in his voice. "He's walking towards the door. Don't worry, you'll be fine."

Gladys dragged Penny behind the bedroom door, and the two of them stood quietly, hardly breathing. Gladys felt a tingle in her fingertips and accepted the fact that she'd cast a spell if she was forced to, although casting a spell on the same person twice in two days could have an adverse effect. It might even bring back Inspector Jameson's memories of seeing Ethel dead in the chapel, but she'd cross that bridge when, or if, she came to it.

A loud banging echoed through the house as the inspector knocked on the door.

Gladys took a deep breath, and felt Penny move next to her.

Barney cleared his throat, and the sound of his footsteps echoed in the hallway as he made his way to the door. "Hello, Sir," he said, as the door creaked open. "What are you doing here?"

"What am I doing here? What are *you* doing here?" said the inspector, his footsteps joining Barney's in the hallway. "Where's Ethel?"

"Erm… she's not here, Sir."

"Where is she, Sergeant Dobkins?"

"I'm not sure, Sir," said Barney.

"Then why are you in a woman's house when she's not here?"

"Erm… I, I'm —" stammered Barney.

The inspector's voice rose in volume. "Has the cat got your tongue, Dobkins? Then maybe I can assist you. You're here because you've been

A MEETING OF MINDS

meddling in things that you shouldn't be meddling in."

"I don't know what you mean, Sir?"

"You know damn well what I mean, Dobkins. I wasn't born yesterday. I had an alert come through to my computer — an alert that told me somebody had been searching for information about something that doesn't concern them… or at least, *shouldn't* concern them…" The inspector's voice took on a menacing tone, "… unless they know something they shouldn't know."

"I don't know what you mean, Sir," said Barney.

Penny moved, and a floorboard squeaked. Gladys put a hand on her granddaughter's arm, urging her to be as still as possible.

"You know fine well what I mean, Dobkins. I set up an alert on the police search system — years ago — for certain terms and names, and it just so happens that you triggered all of them with your frantic searches yesterday. And imagine my surprise when I used the tracking system to trace your car, and found it at the property of the very woman you've been searching the system for," said the inspector. "What are you up to, Sergeant Dobkins? What do you know about Ethel Boyd?"

"Nothing, Sir. I don't know anything about her."

That wasn't a lie, Gladys conceded. Barney knew Ethel was dead, but that was about as far as his knowledge of the woman went.

"Don't mess me around," hissed the inspector. "Why were you searching for crimes committed in nineteen-eighty-seven, and adding Ethel's name to the search criteria? But most fascinating of all, is why you were searching for information about that run down little chapel down by the canal. Why would *that* building, Ethel Boyd, and the year nineteen-eighty-seven, hold any interest for you, Sergeant Dobkins? Answer me!"

"I was… I was…"

"I'll ask again, Dobkins," said the inspector. "Why were you looking for information about Cave Chapel?"

That was a name Gladys hadn't heard for years. In fact, she'd completely forgotten that the building was once known as Cave Chapel.

"I don't know what to tell you, Sir," said Barney.

Barney was faltering. He was no match for the inspector, and what *could* he say? He had no valid reason for being in Ethel Boyd's house. He was going to spill the beans if Gladys didn't do something.

Gladys whispered in Penny's ear as the men continued talking downstairs. "Open a portal in the doorway," she said. "Go to The Haven, and then go back to your boat. I'll meet you there."

"But the inspector will hear," whispered Penny. "Portals make a buzzing sound."

"Just do it," said Granny.

Penny frowned. "What will you do? You shouldn't cast another spell on the inspector, he's still under the influence of the one you put him under yesterday. You could damage him."

Gladys glanced at the photo on the chest of drawers. "Don't worry about me," she said. "I've got an idea."

Penny nodded. She must have known when to trust a wiser witch. "Okay,' she said. "But be careful, Granny."

Penny tip-toed from behind the door, gave Gladys a smile, and cast her spell. The doorway filled with a golden light, and a loud buzzing sound throbbed in the air. She stepped through the portal quickly, the tablet tucked under her arm and an anxious look on her face.

The moment Penny had been completely enveloped in light, the portal closed behind her with a loud popping sound. Penny would be in The Haven, and could simply open another portal which would take her back to Wickford. Gladys could have done the same, but she wasn't going to leave Barney to fend for himself.

"What was that noise?" said the inspector. "Ethel! Are you upstairs?"

Gladys crossed the room quickly, took a quick look at the photograph of Ethel on a beach, and lay down on the bed. Footsteps thudded up the stairs as she muttered a few words and forced the ball of magic which had formed in her chest through every tendon and vein in her body.

A shadow fell across the doorway, and Gladys closed her eyes, hoping the spell would hold.

The inspector's heavy footsteps approached the bed. "You're here?" he said.

CHAPTER TEN

Gladys opened her eyes and yawned. "Oh, hello," she said. "Of course I'm here. I must have nodded off. Is Sergeant Dobkins here? I asked him to come. I didn't think he'd bring you along too."

"You asked him to come?" said the inspector.

"Yes," said Gladys. "He said he'd come alone. I left the front door open incase I was asleep. I do like a snooze after my third cup of tea, you see?"

Gladys pushed herself into a sitting position on the edge of the bed.

"I heard a noise, are you okay?" said the inspector.

"I do snore quite badly," said Gladys. "Sometimes I wake myself up."

"Have you been walking in the hills?" said the inspector. "Your hair looks… windswept."

Gladys attempted to smooth down her hair, but it refused to stay tight against her scalp. Using a photograph as reference for a shape-shifting spell had its problems. "It's my new hair-lacquer," she said. "It's very strong. And expensive. I must have slept awkwardly before it had dried properly."

Barney appeared in the doorway, and Gladys gave him a reassuring smile. He stood still, his face ashen and his eyes wide. Like he'd seen a ghost.

"Did you find any clues, Sergeant Dobkins?" asked Gladys.

"Clues?" said Inspector Jameson. "What's going on here, Dobkins?"

"Erm…" said Barney.

Gladys remembered the pair of saucy knickers in Ethel's drawer. "Don't worry, Sergeant Dobkins," she said. "I'll tell him — as embarrassing as it is for me."

"Tell me what?" said the inspector.

"This is why I asked Sergeant Dobkins to come alone," said Gladys. "I trust him with personal things. He's got a kind face."

"You trust me too, don't you, Ethel?" said the inspector.

The tone of voice the inspector had used put

A MEETING OF MINDS

Gladys on alert. He'd known Ethel well. It was obvious.

"Of course I do," said Gladys, giving the man a reassuring smile. "I didn't want to bother you with silly things like thongs being stolen from my washing line. You've got more important things to be getting on with. I'm sure it's just a local pervert trying to get his filthy kicks. Sergeant Dobkins will get to the *bottom* of it, I'm sure."

The inspector turned to face Barney. "Go into the back garden and have a good look around, if you haven't already. Check for footprints or signs of how somebody got in."

Barney looked at Gladys. Realisation had dawned on his face. He knew he wasn't in the presence of a ghost. "Okay, Sir," he said, raising an eyebrow in Gladys's direction.

When Barney's footsteps had reached the hallway, the inspector looked at Gladys. "Are you sure it's just some random pervert, Ethel? You can't be too careful. He's out of prison now, and I'm the only copper still working here who knows what happened to you."

"Oh, I'm sure," said Gladys, thinking carefully about what she said next. "I caught a glimpse of him climbing over the fence. He was a young man."

"Not him then," said the inspector. "From what I

hear, prison hasn't been kind to him. You have to be careful though, Ethel. I don't know where he went when he was released. All my old contacts are either dead, or living it up in Spain on the money they got paid for the cover-up."

Gladys considered throwing caution to the wind and casting a truth spell on the inspector, but his eyes had the faraway look of somebody already heavily under the influence of magic, and she sensed he was a kind man. She didn't want him to come to any harm. "Do you think he'd come back here? To Wickford?" said Gladys, hoping she was using the right words.

"I doubt it," said the inspector. "He thought he'd killed you. He probably wants to stay as far away from here as possible, and his family won't have him back. Not after the shame he brought on them."

"I suppose not," said Gladys.

The inspector looked carefully at Gladys. Was the spell faltering? "Are you okay, Ethel? You look anxious."

"I'm just tired," said Gladys.

The inspector looked at his shoes. "Listen, Ethel. I came here to bring you something, and I was shocked to find Sergeant Dobkins's car outside. I told him I'd traced him with the car tracking system. I think he knows something he shouldn't. He's been searching the police system for information about you, and about what happened in the chapel. I don't know what he's up to, but I *do* trust the man, he's a good copper. Have you said anything to anyone, Ethel? About what happened to you? Anything that may have got back to the Sergeant?"

Gladys thought quickly. "I went to the chapel yesterday," she said. "And he was there."

"What?" said the inspector.

Gladys smiled. "I was asked to be an organist at a wedding. Gladys Weaver's wedding — she's bought the chapel and she's making it look nice again. Well, when I got there to show them how I could play, Sergeant Dobkins was there too. He's the boyfriend of one of her granddaughters. I was nervous about going in... after what happened, so I mentioned to the Sergeant that something had happened to me in there, in nineteen-eighty-seven. He must have wanted to find out what it was. That's all."

"And you asked him to come here to catch the underwear thief while you were at the chapel?"

"That's right!" said Gladys, happy her story was holding water. "I did! I asked him!"

"You mustn't tell anyone again, Ethel. His father may be dead, but his mother is still alive. She could still cause us a lot of problems. You know what you promised them. You promised you'd never breathe a word of it to anybody in return for thirty years of very generous monthly payments."

"I know," said Gladys. "I was very nervous, you know, stepping into the chapel after all this time, and Sergeant Dobkins was so nice, it just spilled out of me."

"I really don't know why you went in there, Ethel. Among all those bad memories," said Inspector Jameson.

"Gladys is paying well for an organist, and I need the money."

The inspector sighed. "I told you years ago that you should have used that money more wisely. Giving three quarters of your monthly payments to animal shelters was a kind thought, but you could have done so much more with it. You've left yourself financially vulnerable."

"I'll survive," said Gladys. "I always do."

The inspector reached inside his suit pocket. "Here," he said, handing Gladys an envelope. "This is from his mother. She says it's the last you'll hear from her."

Gladys took the envelope and placed it on the bed next to her. "I'll open it later," she said. "Thank you."

The inspector nodded. "Okay. Well, I'd better be going. The further I stay away from you, the better. I don't want to give Sergeant Dobkins any reason to keep searching the computer system. There's nothing there of course, and the file I made is in my safe, but I don't like to think of him stumbling across something he shouldn't. I'm sure he'll find out who's been at your underwear, though, he's nothing if not thorough."

"Do you mind seeing yourself out?" said Gladys. The spell was weakening and Gladys feared any unnecessary movement on her behalf would bring it to an abrupt end.

"Of course," said the inspector. "Take care, Ethel, and take life easy — I'm going away for a few days. I'm flying to Scotland tonight. Three days of salmon fishing will clear the mind, and it seems I need the break. I've been having terrible headaches since yesterday."

Headaches were a normal symptom after being blasted with a powerful witch's spell. He'd be right as rain after a few deep sniffs of the Scottish mountain air. Not like… She stopped herself, pushing the intrusive thoughts from her mind. *He'd be fine too*.

"Enjoy yourself," said Gladys. She remembered the phrase which Norman had always used around his fellow anglers — when he wanted to wish them good luck on their fishing trips. "Tight lines."

The detective thanked her, and Gladys waited until the front door had closed and the inspector's car had pulled out of the driveway, before allowing the spell to completely fade. She hurried down the stairs, with the envelope in her hand.

She peered into the back garden, where Barney was standing in a corner next to a tree, biting his nails. "Come on," she said. "The plot has thickened."

Penny was in *The Spell Weavers* with Willow. She'd phoned Barney the moment she'd arrived back in Wickford through a portal, and Barney drove Gladys straight to the magic shop, seemingly as impatient as she was to find out what was inside the simple white envelope with Ethel's name on the front.

"I've never seen anything like it," said Barney, telling Penny and Willow about Gladys's prowess with a shape-shifting spell. "I really thought it was Ethel for a moment. It was amazing."

There it was. Finally. Admiration for her magic. Gladys smiled. "It was nothing, really. But it worked. The inspector fell for it."

"Open it," said Barney, leaning on the sales counter, a box of fake love potions next to his elbow. "Come on."

Gladys had filled the three of them in with every detail of what had been said in the bedroom, and all that remained to be done was to open the envelope. She slid a nail along the gummed seal and lifted the flap, feeling a little guilty about reading another person's private correspondence. Carefully, she withdrew the single sheet of expensive writing paper, pushed her glasses along her nose, and began to read the handwritten letter as everybody listened.

"Dear Ethel,

So. Thirty years have gone by. You kept your side of the arrangement and we kept ours. I trust the money served you well, and I trust that knowing my son has been locked away for all those years has gone some way towards healing both your physical and emotional pain.

What he did was unforgivable, and as you know, God will be the ultimate judge of his actions. Thinking he had killed you, was, I believe, punishment enough. I believe that the part my husband and I played in locking him away for so long under false pretences, will mean we'll be judged harshly by God too.

Of course, my husband has already met his maker, and I can only pray that God saw the goodness in his heart. What he did in covering the terrible events up was an act of love. He was protecting his family. He was protecting me. In some small way he was protecting our son too — he was too fragile to make his way through life without a vice, and was easily led by people with few morals, leading to his downfall in the eyes of The Lord, and of course, his family. Prison may have been the best place for him.

Make no mistake. I blame you for your part in all of this, too. You should have come to us before threatening him with the law. He was a frightened man, and sometimes frightened men act in ways we'd never imagine they could — especially a man of his standing in the community.

I'm going to attempt to put all of this behind me. I'm no longer young, and will never see my son again. He was disowned by this family the day he let God, us, and himself down. Although he is no longer in prison, he knows he is not welcome in my family. I wish to spend the final years of my life with the children I still have around me, and this brief note will be the last you hear from me. I trust you will respect my privacy in return.

With regards and sorrow,

LHG"

"It sounds like something very bad happened in that chapel," said Willow. "And I think it's safe to say that Ethel's murder is connected to what happened back then."

Penny touched Barney's hand. "You have to get that file from Inspector Jameson's safe," she said. "It will probably hold all the answers."

"I can't," said Barney. "How could I? It's in his office and I don't know the code. There's cameras everywhere, too. I'd be seen, and Inspector Jameson already knows I'm interested in Ethel. I'd be asking for trouble. This all feels very dangerous."

"From what Inspector Jameson said to Granny, it sounds like he's a crooked cop, in on a cover-up" said Willow. "We should just report the whole thing to somebody higher up and let them investigate. We should go back to the chapel, take Ethel's body out of stasis, and reset the last two days."

Gladys shook her head. "No," she said. "Inspector Jameson didn't feel… bad. You have to trust me on that. I'm a good judge of character, and as for reporting it… we can't. I have to get married in two days time. I just have to!"

"Granny," said Penny. "I know how important it is

to you, but surely you can see that we made a mistake. We should have just let the police carry on with their investigation. You can get married on another day."

"No!' said Gladys. "I've booked a band and had a lovely big cake made! The Poacher's Pocket Hotel has stocked up on Pimm's, and Brian has polished his shoes!"

"None of that is hard to do again at a later date," said Willow. "And it's not like you're strapped for cash, is it?"

Gladys close her eyes. She was going to have to say it. The thing that she'd not said out loud yet — even to herself. She took a deep breath. "You know why Aunt Eva can't come through a portal from the Haven? You know why she won't be at my wedding?"

"Because she got ill in this world. She'd be dead within minutes of stepping back into Wickford, where she's not protected by Haven magic. Seconds even," said Penny. "Yes, we know."

Gladys nodded. "Well, I'm sorry to say—"

Willow gasped and pulled Gladys into a tight hug. "You're ill too, aren't you, Granny?" she wept.

Gladys smoothed her granddaughter's hair, and spoke softly. "Not me. No, Willow, not me. It's

Charleston. He didn't want anyone to know. That's the reason he was so happy to be magically trapped in the body of a goat for so long — the thing in his head wouldn't get any bigger. When he came to my cottage on that fateful day and I cast the accidental spell, he only had nine or ten months left, and it's been almost eight."

"But he can't be ill in The Haven," said Barney. "That's what you've always said — people don't get ill there."

"And that's correct," said Gladys, "but dimension travel is a funny old thing, Barney, and one of the frustrating intricacies of it is the fact that the body keeps going in this world. Charleston has spent six-months in The Haven, completely safe from that cruel *thing* in his head. When he steps back into this world, though, it will be six-months more advanced than it was when he left."

"Oh, Granny," said Penny. "You should have told us."

"Charleston wouldn't allow it," said Gladys. "But that's why he hasn't been back to Wickford, and if I want to get married in the chapel my mother always wanted to see me married in, then it has to be on Saturday. If I leave it any later Charleston won't be able to come back to Wickford, and if he risked it, who knows what would happen? I realise it may sound selfish, but I've never really wanted anything in my life as much as I want to honour my mother's wishes."

Barney stood up straight, and an electrifying tingle ran the full length of Gladys's spine as a look of sheer frightening determination spread across the policeman's face.

"You're not selfish, Gladys!" bellowed Barney, his hand forming a fist, and his face as red as his hair. "You're a fine woman who allowed herself to be burnt to death to save the rest of us. You people are my family now, and family helps one another. I'll make sure you get married on Saturday, Gladys. You mark my words! I'm Sergeant Barney Dobkins, and I've got a crime to solve!"

"Barney," said Penny, taking her boyfriend's trembling hand in hers. "That's the most wonderful thing I've ever heard you say. How are you going to do it? How are you going to catch Ethel's killer?"

Barney licked his lips. "I'll… I'll, erm…"

Gladys smiled, her heart lighter than it had been for months. It was true what they said — *a problem shared is a problem halved*. Although Gladys felt that her problem had been quartered and fine diced. She had her family firmly on her side, and that was all she'd ever wanted. "Try and get the file from Inspector Jameson's safe?" she suggested. "He's going to Scotland, so his office will be empty, and we should find out who the initials LHG belong to, *and* try and get access to Ethel's tablet thingy — who knows what information we'll find on that."

"Precisely, Gladys," said Barney. "Just what I was about to say." He lowered his eyes. "I do value your input, but I'd prefer it if people didn't interrupt me in the future." He paused for a moment. "Now, where was I? Oh, yes! We need to do all of *those* things, but I also need to find out if any new arrivals have come to the area recently. If Ethel's murder was anything to do with the man in the letter — the one who's been released from prison, then he'd need somewhere to live. I'll check with the council, estate agents, and private landlords."

"Barney," said Gladys. "With that fine police mind of yours, you'll be a detective in no time at all."

CHAPTER ELEVEN

Gladys handed the tablet to Susie. "Penny and Willow have both tried, but they can't access it. Ethel set a password, and no amount of magic seems to work. It's a tough little thing."

"Don't worry," said Susie. "It will take me a few hours, but I'll get into it. There are people online I can speak to who could get into Fort Knox if they put their mind's to it. What am I looking for?"

"Anything to do with the initials LHG," said Gladys. "And find out if Ethel did online banking. If you could get into her account it would be a great help. If we can find out who was paying her each month, we'll have the case wrapped up by supper time, and the killer in a cell before midnight-snack time."

"LHG," said Susie, raising a bushy eyebrow. "It shouldn't be hard to find somebody with those initials. We know it's a woman who wrote the letter, so that narrows it down. I've got access to the electoral role. I'll see what I can find."

"We've had a good think," said Barney. "And we can't think of anybody in Wickford, or nearby, who has those initials. There's Laura Gambley, but her middle name is Catherine, and she's only twenty-nine. She wasn't even alive in nineteen-eighty-seven."

"Leave it with me," said Susie. "I'll see what I can do."

BARNEY SEEMED NERVOUS, and Gladys wasn't surprised. He was about to help her do something which would finish his career as a police officer if they were caught — *as well* as alerting the whole of the human race to the presence of real life witches and magic. Gladys thought the latter was worse, but Barney seemed to be focusing on the former.

"It will be okay," said Gladys, as Barney turned into High Street and changed gear. "I know exactly what the inspector looks like. His face is firmly etched in my mind, as are his clothes and voice. The shape-shifter spell will be fool proof."

"And you're sure magic will open the safe?" said Barney. "You couldn't even get into a tablet."

"I'm positive," said Gladys. "I've been around a while, you know, Barney. You don't get to… my age, without breaking into a safe or two."

"I don't want to know," said Barney. "Your colourful past is none of my business."

Gladys watched the street go by as she planned the way she'd play the inspector. She'd been around enough police to know how they spoke. If she was forced into a conversation as she walked through the police station, she was sure that nobody would guess they weren't speaking to Inspector Jameson himself. "And you're sure nobody knows he's in Scotland?" said Gladys. "This whole caper relies on that. If that little detail is cleared up, then I literally can't think of anything else that could go wrong. It's a watertight plan."

"I'm sure," said Barney. "He's a private man, and he's coming up to retirement soon. He comes and goes as he pleases, and doesn't really have any good friends on the force. Nobody really notices him. He could be in Papua New Guinea, and nobody would be any the wiser."

A MEETING OF MINDS

Granny watched a small crowd of people standing outside the butcher's shop, and she gasped. She'd been too focused on the murder to think anything else could cause a hiccup on her wedding day, but watching Thomas Ericson being accosted by the same dirty tramp she'd lambasted not three days ago, made her blood run cold. "Pull the car over, Barney!" she said. "Right this moment! That hobo is worrying a member of the band I've booked. Throw him in jail!"

"We've got bigger fish to fry," said Barney. "He's not doing anything illegal anyway. As far as I can see, he's just talking to the busker. Arresting somebody would really draw attention to us when we get to the police station, and we don't want that. There's a lot of paperwork involved."

"He's not talking," said Gladys. "He's shouting! My busker needs his hearing to be in super-duper condition if he's going to play to his full potential at my wedding party, and having a vagabond yelling in his ear could burst an eardrum. You pull this car over right this instance before I cast a spell which will flip this vehicle upside down. *Then* you'll have paperwork to complete."

Barney sighed, and flicked on the indicator. "If you must," he said, pulling over a respectable distance down the road from the crowd. "But I'm parking here. People will think you're in trouble if they see you getting out of a police car."

Gladys clambered out of the car. "Wait here, I won't be long. I'll deal with the insolent little blighter in no time at all!"

She hurried along the pavement, trying her best to avoid stepping on the cracks. It was the only superstition Gladys paid any heed to, and it had caused numerous arguments with Norman when he'd installed crazy paving in the back garden. Her dancing had improved, but she'd still made her husband rip them up and replace them with concrete.

As Gladys neared the butcher's shop, she heard raised voices. "Leave me alone!" shouted Thomas. "You're mad! Of course I'm not!"

Gladys pushed her way through the spectators, ignoring their protests. "What on earth are you doing?" said Gladys, looking the dirty bearded man up and down.

"Nothing to do with you," he said. He took an open can of cider from his pocket and took a swig. "Unless you're one of them too!"

"One of what?' said Gladys. "You're making no sense, man!"

"A ghost!" said the tramp. "I've already seen one! Are you one too? Come here, let me feel you!"

A MEETING OF MINDS

Gladys scowled as she pushed the man's hand away. "Get your dirty paws off me, you drunk old fool. You've got a filthy bandage on one of them, who knows what infections you've picked up! Anyway — I thought I told you to get lost the other day. Go on, get out of here, get back under your stone and leave people alone."

"I tried to go home," said the man. "But I couldn't. I couldn't find it. I just kept on wandering until I came back here. But I like it here in town. There's no ghosts."

"Of course you can't find your way home if you're always drunk, but if you don't wander your way off down the street this instant," said Gladys, "*you'll* be a ghost by the time I've finished with you!"

The man scowled at Gladys. "I hate this town," he said, making the sign of the cross on his chest. "It's got no morals."

"You've got no morals!" said Gladys. "Drinking in the street in broad daylight and accosting poor buskers. Now go on, shoo! And give me your name! If you get into any more trouble I want to be able to tell the police who to arrest!"

He gave Gladys a dejected look. "They call me The Bear."

Gladys studied him. Big and hairy, and he smelt

too. It was a fitting name. "Well, Mister Bear, I suggest you get going, or I'll make you tell me your real name!"

The Bear sighed. "I know when I'm not wanted," he said. He gave the crowd a menacing stare and began stumbling along the pavement, placing his can back in the pocket of his thick overcoat.

"Wait," said a voice. "Don't forget these."

The well-built butcher stood in the doorway of his shop, holding out a paper bag. "Scraps of liver and kidney, just like you asked for."

"Thank you, Sir," said The Bear, taking the bag. "God bless you."

"You can thank me by not causing scenes outside my shop," said the butcher, slamming the door as he went back inside his shop.

Gladys looked at Thomas with concern. "Will you still be able to play on Saturday?" she said. "I know how sensitive you musical types can be, and he was very aggressive towards you. Do you still feel like you have talent?"

"I'm fine," said Thomas, nodding his thanks to a lady who dropped a coin in his box. "Me and the band are looking forward to it, we've got a real treat of a playlist lined up for you. It'll be a good night. I promise."

A MEETING OF MINDS

BARNEY PARKED behind the police station. The carpark wasn't very large, but he managed to find a secluded spot behind the wheelie bins which brimmed with paper and styrofoam cups.

"Are you sure you can pull this off, Gladys?' said Barney. "If we get caught, who knows what will happen."

"Have faith," said Gladys. "And if the worse comes to the worse, I'll set off an EMP so large this town won't know what's hit it."

Barney shrugged. "In for a penny, in for a pound. I said I'd help, so let's get on with it."

Gladys closed her eyes and imagined Inspector Jameson's face. His body and clothes would be easy to mimic, but the face would give her away if she didn't capture the most important details. She pictured his nose, thin at the top, but widening into a ball above the nostrils, lined with the thin veins of a man who drank. His eyes were easy to capture — bright and inquisitive, with lids that drooped when he spoke.

When Gladys was sure the image in her head was the one she wanted her body to portray, she took a deep breath and cast her spell. She watched herself in the sun-visor vanity mirror as her face shimmered and shifted, her blue perm being replaced with thinning grey hair.

"Woah!" said Barney. "You look just like him! This is weird."

"I'm a man!" said Gladys, testing the voice. She'd mimicked Ethel's voice perfectly, and judging by Barney's reaction, she'd done the same with the inspector. "A big ol' man! I've never been a man before, Barney! I like it… I feel so… powerful!"

"Don't call me by my first name," said Barney. "Call me Sergeant from this moment forward, and remember to stay close to me. I'll take you to his office, and don't speak to anybody unless they speak to you. I want to be in and out as quickly as possible."

Gladys nodded, her hand wandering along her corduroy clad thigh.

"What are you doing?" said Barney. "Take your hand off that! It's not yours!"

"It's not his either," said Gladys, giving a gentle squeeze. "It's a facsimile copy of his body — and anyway, it's nothing to write home about. I won't be touching it again."

Barney took a deep breath. "If you've quite finished molesting yourself, we should go. The sooner we get this over with, the better."

Gladys nodded. "Lead the way, Sergeant."

CHAPTER TWELVE

Gladys felt like she was nine inches taller. It was obvious from the way she no longer needed to angle her neck painfully as she looked up at Barney, that she was taller on the outside, but Gladys felt taller on the inside, too.

She swelled with a pride she'd never before experienced as Barney punched the code into the door lock, and as she entered the police station, she realised what was happening to her — she was infected with male —privilege and toxic-masculinity, and boy, it felt good. Too good.

Barney whispered one last warning. "This is the custody suite. Don't say a word unless you have to, just follow me."

Gladys gave Barney a manly slap on his back, her new-found masculinity a drug which gave her more confidence than she'd ever imagined. She was a man now, unshackled from the chains which kept women in their place. The world was hers for the taking. And she wanted it. All of it.

Gladys walked alongside Barney as they passed the custody desk, heading for the door which would take them into the beating heart of the station. The place where men made important decisions.

The custody desk sergeant greeted them in a tired voice. "Morning, guys."

Guys. What a powerful word. A word endowed with privilege and power.

Gladys smiled at the desk sergeant. She could tell he'd been on duty all night, and was probably looking forward to getting to the golf course or gentleman's club when he finished his shift. Or perhaps he would go hunting. He looked like a hunter.

"Morning, Harry," said Barney, hurrying through the suite. "Busy night?"

"Just the normal," said Harry. "Local teens smoking cannabis, and a drunk driver."

Gladys knew she must answer too. Harry had greeted them both, it would seem rude if she remained silent. "Yo, Harry," she said, surprised at how easily she had slipped into the role of Detective Inspector. "Did anyone fall down the stairs on their way to a cell? You know what I'm saying — nudge-nudge, wink-wink."

Harry took a step backwards. "Urm... no, Sir. There are no stairs to the cells, and we take health and safety very seriously. There's never been an accident on my shift." He put his hand to his head. "Touch wood."

"Perhaps it's about time there was," said Gladys, offering Harry a conspiratorial wink. "All work and no play makes Jack a dull boy, if you know what I mean — nudge-nudge, wink-wink."

"Are you okay, Sir?" said Harry.

"He's just having a joke," said Barney, putting a hand on Glady's back and forcing her towards the door.

"I don't find it particularly funny if I'm honest, Sir," said Harry. "Those days are long behind us, and I don't feel it's appropriate to joke about them. I take my job very seriously."

Gladys noted the cameras on the walls. *They were being recorded.* No wonder Harry wouldn't open up to his superior.

"I get you, Harry," said Gladys, tapping the side of her nose, and winking again. "We've got to be careful these days. Those cell doors are very heavy, imagine the damage one of them could do to a perp's hand if it was accidentally slammed on it. I know where you're coming from — the prisoner's safety must always come first, nudge-nudge, wink-wink."

Barney punched the code into the door lock, and pulled it open. "Come on, Sir," he said. "Harry's tired, he's not in the mood for your jokes."

Gladys allowed herself to be ushered through the door and into the corridor beyond, and frowned as Barney moved his face close to hers.

"What the hell are you playing at?" said Barney, his anger barely disguised. "That's not how police speak to each other. Don't say a word from this moment forward. Do you understand?"

Gladys wondered whether she should land a manly fist on Barney's nose. Her toxic-masculinity seemed to be playing havoc with her normally mild feminine temper. No wonder men liked wrestling so much, she'd have liked nothing more than to have stripped off her jacket and shirt, ripped Barney's clothes from his body, oiled both Barney and herself up, and grappled out their differences — right there, on the cheap carpet tiles.

Barney was stick thin, though, and he looked very weak — she'd have him in a half-nelson before he could squeal his defeat. The fight would be unfair. She took a calming breath and realigned her chakras.

"Chill out, bucko. I've got this. No more talking. I get it. Jeez."

"Stop speaking like that," said Barney. "You sound like an American television detective. Inspector Jameson is quieter than that. He hardly speaks to anybody unless he has to. You'll raise suspicions."

A door on the left wall of the corridor creaked open, and a portly man in uniform stepped through it, peering along the corridor. "Ah, Sergeant Dobkins," he said. "I thought I heard your voice. Step inside my office, would you? I need you to do something for me this afternoon."

"Can it wait, Sir?" said Barney, "I need to—"

Barney's superior shook his head. "Now, please, Sergeant. It needs to be sorted out immediately. We need to send a representative to a funeral, and with your height and good looks, you'll do our little force proud. Step inside my office and I'll fill you in on the details."

"I'll be right in, Sir," said Barney.

"Good," said the big man, stepping back inside his office. "I'm sure Inspector Jameson has more important things to do than talk to you in a corridor."

Barney looked at Gladys, and spoke in a whisper. "End of the corridor, turn right, go up the stairs and turn left. His office is on the right. His name is on the door and it will be open. It always is. I'll meet you there when I'm finished with the boss."

Gladys gave Barney a mock salute. "Don't worry about me, I'll find it."

Barney gave Gladys a concerned frown and stepped into the office, closing the door behind himself.

Gladys straightened her shirt and pulled back her shoulders, pushing her chest out. She felt like Inspector Jameson was an alpha male, and she wanted to make sure his reputation was kept fully intact. If she walked through the station like a frightened mouse, the other alpha males would turn on her, and when the Inspector came back from Scotland, he'd be shocked to find out he'd been demoted to a worthless beta.

Not on her watch. While she was borrowing the Inspector's likeness, she was going to treat it with the upmost respect. The respect it deserved.

Gladys strolled along the corridor, but something felt wrong. She'd seen Inspector Jameson walk, and he was no stroller — he was a man who strutted. She accessed her inner soundtrack. Gladys enjoyed playing music in her mind while she walked, and *The Bee Gees — Staying Alive* was the perfect song to strut to.

She lifted her head high, and took long bouncing steps as she recalled Barney's directions. She turned right at the end of the corridor, ignoring the people who were hunched over computers in the open-plan office, and bounded up the steps. She took them two at a time, mimicking the way Norman had ascended steps until the gout had began *really* taking its toll.

With the Bee Gees blasting in her head, Gladys reached the top of the stairs and ran a hand through her greying hair, wondering if men washed their barnets as often as women did. Now, what had Barney said? Right at the top of the stairs. Or had it been left? Gladys went left, it felt more natural, and there was an inviting aroma of coffee coming from that direction.

She peered at the name plates on the doors, looking for the correct office. None of them bore Inspector Jameson's name, and she was about to turn around, realising she should have gone right at the top of the stairs, when she saw it — through an open doorway — ripe, full, and begging for the big hairy hand of a burly alpha male.

Gladys looked at her hand, and then she gazed at the female constable's bottom again.

She was bending over a table in a little kitchen,

speaking to three men and another woman, who sat with mugs in front of them, eating biscuits.

For a moment, Gladys wished she had been born a man. It was exhilarating to feel the male-privilege boiling her blood, and she knew she'd be a fool if she didn't experience at least one of the things that men did on a regular basis. She wouldn't be in Inspector Jameson's body for long, and she was going to make the most of the temporary perks afforded her by being a man.

What was it Barney had said? Inspector Jameson didn't have many friends in the police station? Gladys would see about that. By the time Inspector Jameson got back from Scotland, he'd be a hero among the other men. Without a shadow of a doubt — a certain inspector's Christmas card list was about to get impressively longer.

Gladys took a deep breath and centred her masculinity, imagining the whoops and hollers she'd receive from the other men in the room when she slapped the firm rump. No, slapping didn't feel like the correct word for what she wanted to do. *Walloping* was more like it.

She strutted into the room, enjoying the smell of percolated coffee, and smiling as she spotted the digestive biscuits on the counter. She liked digestives. She'd have one when she was done.

Gladys swung her arm like a pendulum, remembering to move it from the shoulder for maximum effect. The air swished as her hand sliced through it, and her palm tingled pleasantly as she made contact with the fleshy buttocks. "Fetch me some doughnuts, you fine little filly!" she bellowed.

She lifted her hand and grinned, anticipating the admiring high-fives she was about to receive from her fellow men.

Her breath left her in a gasp as the first man flew at her, knocking her against the kitchen counter as another man forced her hand up her back.

"How dare you!" yelled the female constable, balling her hand into a fist.

"Leave it, Shaz," said the other woman, grabbing her friend's arm as she aimed her fist at Gladys's face. "He's not worth getting yourself in trouble over."

"What are you playing at?" said one of the men, staring at Gladys.

"I... I'm not sure," said Gladys.

She *wasn't* sure, but she was beginning to understand. She realised with a terrible wrenching in her gut that what she'd just done was terrible. Of course it was terrible — she'd assaulted a woman! She'd acted terribly since she'd entered the police station.

She remembered what her mother had told her when she was young. *A spell cast in stress is not one to impress.*

Gladys had been casting too many spells, and with concerns growing within her about Charleston's health, her wedding, and Ethel's murder — she was surely going to mess up sooner or later. The shape-shifting spell had not been pure. She'd been far too worried when she'd cast it. The magic was tangled — changing her personality, muddying her mind, and bringing her deep-seated beliefs bubbling to the surface.

Gladys gasped. She'd acted like the one of the things she hated the most. "Oh my goodness," she said. "I'm a misogynist!"

The woman who'd been on the receiving end of the misogynistic attack gazed at Gladys. "That wasn't like you, Sir," she said. "You're normally so kind to me. Are you okay? You said you had a bad headache yesterday. You don't look well."

Footsteps hurried along the hallway outside. "Inspector Jameson?" came a voice. *Barney's voice.*

"In here," said one of the men.

Barney stepped into the kitchen. "What's

happened," he said, staring at the scene, his pupils dilated and his face white. "Why are you manhandling Inspector Jameson?"

The man holding Gladys's arm looked at Barney. "I'll tell you what happened. He came in here—"

"Nothing happened," said the young woman. "It was a misunderstanding. I think he needs to sit down, Sergeant. Why don't you take him to his office?"

"Are you sure, Sharon?" said one of the men.

"I'm sure," said Sharon. She looked at Barney. "Nothing happened, Sergeant. The Inspector must be poorly."

The two men reluctantly released their grip on Gladys, and Barney led her from the room.

"We need to hurry," said Gladys. "I can't hold the spell for much longer. I feel weak."

"Can you open the safe?" said Barney, pulling Gladys behind him.

Gladys nodded. "I think so. That's a simple spell. The shape-shifting spell is the one I'm struggling with."

"You'd better hold it," said Barney, guiding Gladys towards an office door. "Members of the public aren't allowed up here. I'll get in a world of trouble if you suddenly change back into yourself."

Barney opened the door and pushed Gladys into

the room. The office was small, and contained the bare minimum of furniture required for an inspector to be able to do his job properly.

A desk with a seat on either side filled most of the floor space, and a dehydrated plant stood in a corner, looking lonely and unloved. The inspector's desk was as barren as the rest of the room, with only a computer and a pen-pot on the cheap wooden surface.

A filing cabinet filled one of the corners behind the desk, and on top of it, beneath a small pile of books, was the safe. Heavy bolts secured it to the wall, and the worn green paint around the code-dial told Gladys it was an old piece of equipment. She wondered what secrets had been hidden in it over the years, and smiled inwardly as she remembered opening the safe in her father's study when she'd been a young girl, eager to test her blossoming magic.

She'd never told her father she'd been in his safe and discovered his secret, and she'd *certainly* not told her mother — who luckily for her husband, was not the sort of woman who'd have snooped through a man's private belongings.

Gladys had known, even at that young age, that some secrets could destroy marriages, and being married to a man who was a fully paid-up member of *The Wickford Fine Wine Tasting Club*, was not something her beer swilling mother would have suffered for long. *"Wine is for the French and the bourgeoisie,"* her mother had told her, *"especially red wine. Never trust a working class man who drinks it — he'll break your heart, have teeth like coal, and empty the bank account."*

"Well," said Barney. "Can you open it?"

Gladys brought herself back to the present and wiggled her fingers. "Of course I can," she said. "I'll have it open in seconds." She stood in front of the safe and laid her hand on the cool metal surface. The spell was simple, and almost immediately after casting it, the dial span left and right — the lock clicking as the magic did its work. "There," she said, pulling the door open. " I told you it would be easy."

Barney reached into the safe as Gladys sat down. She was beginning to feel a little giddy, and she knew the shape-shifting spell would not last for much longer. "Hurry," she said. "Just find the file. I need to get out of here and have a cup of sweet tea."

"We're not taking the file with us," said Barney. "He'd notice it was missing. I'll take some photos of it with my phone."

Gladys sighed. Her vision was becoming blurry. She needed to relieve some of the pressure on what she called her centre of magic — the tight little ball

A MEETING OF MINDS

that swelled in her chest like a swallowed golf ball whenever she cast a spell. She eased back on the magic, allowing the shape-shifter spell to weaken. Not enough that someone from afar would know something peculiar was happening, but just enough to allow her own eye colour to shine through, and allow the spell to recuperate a little.

"Here it is!" said Barney, dropping a red folder on the desk. "A genuine nineteen-eighties's police file, complete with rubber band and old paper smell."

Gladys glanced at the folder. She could hardly make out what the black marker pen scrawled writing on the cover said, let alone the small hand writing that she squinted at as Barney opened the file.

With his phone in hand, Barney took a photograph of the first page. He took a corner of the yellowed paper between finger and thumb, and just as he was about to turn the page, the office door handle clicked, and then moved. "Somebody's here," he hissed. "Act casual!"

The door swung open and Sharon stepped into the office, a mug in her hand, and a look of concern on her face.

"Don't you know how to knock?" said Barney.

"I'm sorry," said the young constable. "I thought I'd bring the inspector a cup of tea, he looked like he needed one." She looked at Gladys. "Are you feeling okay, Sir?"

Gladys strengthened the shape-shifter spell, the magic flowing slowly through her limbs, warming her flesh. She cleared her throat. "I'm fine, thank you, and I'm sorry about what happened in the kitchen. I don't know what I was thinking."

"It's forgotten," said Sharon, approaching the desk, the tea held out before her. "I knew you couldn't have been feeling well, Sir. You'd never have done anything like that otherwise. It must be the stress of the job. Maybe you need a break — didn't you mention something about going to Scotland?"

"Erm, yes," said Gladys. "I'm going tomorrow. For a few days. The break will do me good."

Sharon leaned across the desk, placing the mug in front of Gladys, who shuddered as guilt twisted her insides. She relaxed a little as she realised that the guilt was a good thing. It acted as positive reinforcement for her long held opinions on the patriarchy. It was Sharon who had *been* tampered with by a man — yet it was Sharon who was making tea for the male bastard who'd been guilty of the tampering.

It was a travesty and an injustice, and Gladys was happy to note that Sharon seemed to be coming to the same conclusion. Her eyes were widening with shock, and she took a quick step backwards, the mug tipping as she snatched her hand towards her open mouth.

Hot tea flowed over the folder in a mini tidal wave of brown fluid, and Sharon gasped. "I'm so sorry!" she said. "But something happened, Sir. Your eyes — they changed colour! I'm sure of it!"

Barney snatched the folder from the desk in an attempt to save it, but Gladys could see it was too late. The old paper was sodden, and Gladys doubted any amount of drying, or magical intervention, would save the information recorded on it all those years ago.

"My eyes?" said Gladys, sending a surge of magic through her body, ensuring the spell was strong.

"I don't know, Sir," said Sharon, shaking her head. "I could have sworn they changed colour."

"Shock?" said Gladys. "What I did to you was awful, maybe it's you who needs a cup of tea?"

Sharon nodded. "Of course, Sir. Eyes don't change colour — I know that! I'm sorry about the file, I'll print another one off for you if you like?"

Gladys didn't bother telling the poor girl that the file was one of a kind. "It's okay," she said. "It wasn't important."

When Sharon left the room, Barney sighed. "It's

ruined," he said, holding the dripping file over a waste paper bin.

"Just put it back in the safe," said Gladys. "You took one photograph. That will have to do."

"He'll know somebody's been in the safe," said Barney. "We can't put a soaking wet file in there!"

Gladys waved a hand. "There," she said. "Now it's not wet. I can't do magic which will bring washed away ink back, but I can dry paper. Put it back in the safe. He'll assume it's faded over time, and if he doesn't — who cares? He can't report it to anybody."

Barney shrugged and placed the file back in the safe. He closed the door, ensuring it was locked. "Okay. Let's get out of here," he said, "and Gladys… what exactly did happen in the kitchen?"

CHAPTER THIRTEEN

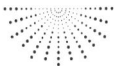

"You slapped a young female constable's bottom?" said Penny. "Now I've heard it all."

"I've told the story," said Gladys. "I won't speak of it again. As far as I'm concerned, it's history. Anyway, I won't be casting any shape-shifting spells for a while. They're tiring."

Willow topped Gladys's cup up with hot fresh tea, and added a splash of milk. "There you go, Granny," she said. "One more of those and you'll be as right as rain again."

Gladys smiled. "Thank you, dear. Now, let's have a look at that photo that Barney took."

Penny placed her phone where they could all see it. Barney had sent the picture he'd taken of the file to

Penny's phone, and headed off to the funeral he'd been ordered to attend.

"Barney says there's nothing revelatory in the photo," said Penny. "It's just an intro to the rest of the file."

"Which was ruined by tea," said Granny. She sipped her drink. "Which is such a shame. I hate to think of tea in stressful terms, it's always been a great calming force in my life." She picked Penny's phone up and narrowed her eyes. "My glasses are good," she said. "But I can't read that. It's far too small."

A boat chugged by on the canal, and the bow-wave rolled into the *Water Witch's* private mooring, rocking the boat gently. Gladys waited for her tea to settle in the cup before taking another sip and passing the phone to Penny. "You read it, dear."

Penny frowned. "It's like Barney said. It's a cover note — just a short paragraph." She moved the phone nearer her face. "*This is a confession of sorts,*" she read.

"A guilty conscience," said Gladys. "Laid bare."

Penny continued. "*I was on the sidelines of an incident which occurred in nineteen-eighty-seven. The Wickford police force was corralled into a cover-up of sorts by a powerful person. Although the criminal concerned was punished for his crime, he was charged with a crime far more serious than the one he had, in reality, committed. The parents of the man in question helped secure their son's false imprisonment, and both continued with their high-level careers, with no evidence of the crime their son had committed ever making its way into the public domain. The following document outlines the incidents in chronological order, and the names of the people involved in the cover-up.*"

Penny put her phone down.

"Is that it?" said Gladys. "We know most of that from the letter that Ethel was supposed to receive."

"That's it," said Penny. "It seems like your trip to the police station was wasted."

"And it tired me out so much, too," said Gladys. "I feel like I'm made of lead. I'm not used to casting so many spells in such a short time frame. I've spent too many months in The Haven. I'm not used to being in the mortal world. The magic feels so weak here."

"Why don't you pop back to The Haven?" suggested Willow. "You'll feel better the moment you step through a portal, and you must be missing Charleston."

"I'm supposed to be getting married the day after tomorrow," said Gladys. "I can't go back to Charleston and tell him what's going on here, he'll be excited about slipping his ring over my finger on Saturday — I don't want him to worry that the wedding won't be going ahead. And I can't lie to him either. I *won't* lie to him."

"Why don't you go and visit Eva instead?" suggested Penny. "Me and Willow will go and find out if Susie has got into the tablet yet, and if anything else important happens, I'll open a portal and come straight to The Haven and tell you. You need your magic recharged, Granny. You're not a young witch anymore, and you'll need all your power to cast a beautification spell over the chapel."

"If your magic weakens too much, the spells you've already cast over the chapel might fail," said Willow. "We don't want Ethel's body coming out of stasis before we find out who killed her."

"And you cast a spell which stops people approaching the chapel," said Penny. "Go on, Granny. Go to The Haven for an hour or two and regain your strength."

Gladys sighed. Like it or not, Penny was right — she wasn't a young witch anymore. She didn't consider herself *old*, but she certainly wasn't in the first flush of youth any longer. She could begrudgingly accept that. "Fine," she said. "I'll go and see my

A MEETING OF MINDS

sister, but if anything happens, you come and get me okay?"

The girls nodded.

"Do you mind if I use your bathroom door, Penelope?" said Gladys. She'd been brought up to always ask permission before using somebody's doorway as a portal, and she was proud of her manners.

"Of course you can," said Penny.

Gladys struggled to her feet — she *was* very tired. A trip to The Haven would be a welcome elixir, and Eva did make a wonderful cup of tea. She stood before the small doorway, pictured where she wanted the portal to open in The Haven, and cast her spell.

EVA HARDLY RAISED an eyebrow as her sister stepped out of the light and through her kitchen door. "Gladys!" she said. "How lovely to see you. I thought you'd forgotten about us commoners since taking up residence in that fancy castle of yours."

"I'll always have time for the simple things in life," said Gladys, taking a seat at the large table. "And there's nobody simpler than you."

Gladys sniffed the air. Her sister was baking flapjacks.

"You look tired," said Eva. "Cuppa?"

Gladys nodded, and watched her sister making the tea. She was happy that Eva was in her eighty-nine year old body, and hadn't taken on the form of her younger self. Although Gladys would never utter the words out loud, she'd always been jealous of her sister's figure when they'd both been younger. Eva had always seemed... more in proportion than herself.

Eva placed the large green teapot between them, and slid a cup across the table. "Help yourself," she said, ever the gracious hostess. "And tell me about your wedding arrangements. Are you all ready for Saturday?"

"Sort of," said Gladys. "I do wish you could come, you know that, don't you?"

"I'd croak within seconds of arriving in Wickford," said Eva. "Then you'd be having one wedding and a funeral. I'm happy enough just knowing you're getting married in the chapel that Mum was married in, and I'm sure you'll show me the photographs."

"*If* I get married in the chapel," said Gladys, spooning sugar into her cup.

"What do you mean *if*?" said Eva. "That's the whole reason you're not getting married here — in The Haven — so you can finally honour Mother's wishes!"

"Something happened in the chapel," said Gladys. "Something terrible, and I think I've done the wrong thing about it. You know how emotional I can get in the grip of a panic."

If Gladys had ever been asked to list both her strong and her weak qualities, the fact that she got emotional in a panic would have been at the very top of both columns, but in the instance of Ethel's murder — she was working directly from the weak points column. She wished she could turn back the clock and allow the police to continue with their investigation of Ethel's murder. It seemed that her *investigation* was getting her nowhere.

"What's happened?" said Eva. "I bet it's got something to do with bats, hasn't it?"

"What is it with bats?" said Gladys. "No! It's not bats. Somebody was murdered in the chapel, and I think my response was over-zealous."

Eva sipped her tea. "Let me get us both a flapjack from the oven, and then you can tell me all about it. I love a good murder yarn."

WHEN GLADYS HAD FINISHED SPEAKING, she sat back in her seat and sighed. Saying it all out loud had made her realise how foolish she'd been. She'd never had a chance of finding out who'd killed Ethel. She should have left it to the police. Perhaps they'd have solved it by now, and her wedding would be going ahead as planned.

"I think your response was perfectly understandable in the situation," said Eva, much to Gladys's surprise. "You've finally found another man stupi— lucky enough to marry you, and you felt threatened. I wouldn't have acted like you, of course. I'd have simply rearranged the wedding date and allowed the police to complete their *very* important work, but as you've already noted — you're governed by your emotions."

"I can't rearrange the date," said Gladys, spinning her cup in its saucer. "If I tell you something, can we just skate over it and not discuss it further?"

Eva put her cup down and tilted her head. "Of course," she said. "I promise."

A promise from Eva was as good as Gladys needed. She forced the words from her mouth. They were hard to speak. Although she knew Charleston would be safe in The Haven, she hated to think of anything bad happening to him.

She frowned. "Charleston can't make many more visits to Wickford," she said. "His mortal body is failing, and time is running out for him in the other world. If I don't get married in that chapel on Saturday, I won't be getting married there at all. He can't risk waiting another two weeks, let alone the time it will take to cancel all the invitations and rearrange everything. He'd die the second he passed through the portal."

Eva put her hand on Gladys's. "Charleston and I have something in common then," she said. "Well. You'd better find out who killed Ethel. She won't care how many spells you've cast, and how much you've complicated things. She's dead. You must concentrate on the living, like Mum always told us."

"We think alike,' said Gladys. "But I don't know what to do next."

"Did you bring the letter?" said Eva. "The one that was meant for Ethel? Maybe a fresh pair of eyes will throw some light on it."

Gladys reached into her pocket and retrieved the envelope, she slid the letter from it and handed it to her sister. She hoped Eva was speaking in analogies, because her cataract clouded eyes were about as fresh as the ideas Gladys had about going any further towards solving Ethel's murder.

Eva read it slowly, her mouth silently forming the words as her eyes danced over the paper. "LHG," she said. "When you told me about the letter, the initials rang a bell somewhere in the back of my mind, but seeing it written down on paper is like having Big Ben clanging in my head." She put the letter down. "I know who wrote this, Gladys. I know who LHG is."

CHAPTER FOURTEEN

*G*ladys was exhilarated. Her magic felt fresh, and her bones had stopped aching. She felt ten years younger, and as she stumbled through the portal and into the *Water Witch,* she shouted the news at the top of her voice. "I've blown the case wide open!" she yelled.

"We know who LHG is!' shouted Willow.

Gladys blinked. Barney and Susie had joined Willow and Penny, and the four of them sat around the table staring at her.

"I know who LHG is, too!" said Gladys. "What time did you find out? I found out fifteen minutes ago."

"I found out about twenty minutes ago," said Susie. "Not that it matters. It's not a competition."

Barney scowled. "I found out about half an hour

ago, but I couldn't get back here to tell anybody. If it *is* a competition. I won. Hands down."

Gladys controlled her irrational rage. The first step to controlling rage was to know whether it was irrational or not, and Gladys considered herself a good judge of her own character. "I really don't think it matters who found out first," she said. "It simply matters that we know. The burning question is why you didn't come and tell me, Penelope? You promised that you'd come through a portal if there was any news."

"I was going to," said Penny. "But Susie and Barney only just got here. We were comparing notes."

Gladys nudged Rosie out of the comfy wicker chair and sat down. The cat gave a mewl of protestation, but leapt up onto Willow's lap and settled down.

"How did you two find out?" said Gladys. "Eva told me. She used to work for her, over forty years ago, as a cook. She remembered the initials." She looked at Susie. "You go first. How do you know who LHG is?"

Susie held up the tablet. "I got into this. It was easy with a little help from the internet, and as you suspected, Gladys, Ethel banked online. She obviously didn't trust her memory because there's a little file on here containing all her passwords, and even her credit card pin numbers. I found out who was paying her, and how much. Ethel was receiving five thousand pounds each month, and the amount never changed. Five grand is a lot now, but the payments go back thirty years. Five grand was an *awful* lot back then."

"She got paid a lot to keep quiet about something," said Gladys. She turned her attention to Barney. "What about you? How did you find out?"

Barney picked up a white booklet from the tabletop. A black cross on the front, and the sombre font used for the typeset told Gladys what it was without reading the words. "A funeral order of service," she said.

Barney nodded. "She said in the letter to Ethel that her husband was dead, she didn't say how recently though. He only died last week, and the reason my boss wanted one of the force at the funeral was as a mark of respect for all the work he did. He was a judge in the eighties, you see. He put a lot of criminals behind bars."

"Including his son," said Gladys. She took Ethel's letter from her pocket and read from it. "*What he did was unforgivable, and as you know, God will be the ultimate judge of his actions. Thinking he had killed you, was, I believe, punishment enough. I believe that the part my husband and I played in locking him away for so long under false pretences, will mean we'll be judged harshly by God too."*

"He locked his own son away," said Willow.

Gladys folded the letter and nodded. "On false charges. Lord Benjamin Green was a corrupt judge. Let's see what his wife has to say for herself. Lady Helen Green has a lot of explaining to do."

"What's the plan?" said Barney. "The woman has just buried her husband, and nobody knows Ethel is dead. We're assuming Ethel's death is something to do with Lady Green's son, but I checked with all the relevant agencies and nobody has moved to town since he was released from prison."

"Murderers don't have to live in the town they kill in," said Gladys. "In fact it's probably best for their liberty if they don't."

"I know," said Barney. "I'm just saying we're assuming an awful lot of things with no evidence apart from a cover-up almost thirty years ago. We don't know what was covered up, and we don't know why. We can't just turn up at Lady Green's house and demand answers."

Gladys smiled. "*You're* not coming with us, Barney. This is a job for witches. If we need to make the good Lady's tongue wag, then no amount of police presence is going to help. It'll be down to good old fashioned magic. Questioning Lady Helen Green is a job for me and my granddaughters. And don't worry, I'll be sensitive to her recent loss, but I intend to have all the answers I need by this evening."

THE KEY-CODE ENTRY security gates posed no problem for a car containing three witches, and Willow opened them with a simple spell, smiling as lilac sparks flowed from her fingers. The lane beyond the gates was more like a road than a driveway, and Gladys gunned the Range Rover's engine, ignoring the polite sign which asked visitors to drive safely.

The Green's mansion was set in impressive grounds. Ancient oak trees dominated the surrounding hills, and the large expanses of lawns were neatly cut, with barely a weed to be seen. Gladys respected a well kept outside space, but she did not respect wealthy people who covered up the crimes of their children. Even if they were grieving.

She followed the driveway lined with beech trees until the large house came into view. A single car was parked in the spacious gravelled area in front of the house, and Gladys brought the Range Rover to a halt next to the sleek black Jaguar.

She opened her door quickly and stepped out of the car. "Let's do this," she said, straightening her blouse and patting down her hair. She was at the home of a Lady after all. She had to look the part.

The large home was built from local stone, and the steps which led to the main entrance were decorated with potted shrubs. Gladys wiped her shoes on the boot scraper, and pressed the doorbell, wondering how many servants a house of such grandeur would require to ensure it ran smoothly.

The door opened slowly, and Gladys stared at the woman before her. She was certainly no servant, and if she was, she was an impeccably dressed servant. The woman's red eyes, and the tissue tucked into the cuff of what looked to be a cashmere sweater, told Gladys what she needed to know. "I'm sorry for your loss, Lady Green," she said, offering a half courtesy.

The elderly lady looked at them in turn. "Who are you?" she said. "How did you get through the security gates? I made sure they were locked. I wanted to be alone today."

"The gates were easy to get though, and we've come to speak to you about your son," said Gladys. "And Ethel Boyd. Can we come in please?"

A MEETING OF MINDS

A tendon in Lady Green's neck tightened, and Gladys noted the spark of anxiety that flashed briefly in her eyes. She look directly at Gladys. "I knew this day would come," she said. "The day I was finally confronted for my sins." She looked Gladys up and down. "But I didn't expect to be explaining myself to a tatty old woman and her two sidekicks. Why on earth do you think I'm going to tell you three anything?"

"Don't speak to my grandmother like that," said Penny.

Gladys laid a calming hand on her granddaughter's arm. "Lady Green," she said. "Believe me when I say that I'm terribly sorry you've lost your husband, but also believe me when I say I'm going to get to the bottom of what happened in nineteen-eighty-seven. You can either speak to us, or you can speak to the police — and I don't mean the police who were involved in the cover-up."

Lady Green dropped her shoulders, and her face crumpled. "Who put you up to this?" she said. "How can you possibly know anything about what happened all those years ago?"

Gladys took the letter which Lady Green had written from her pocket. "This is your writing, isn't it?"

As Lady Green stared at the letter, Gladys knew the elderly woman was beaten. She also sensed that the well dressed woman was filled with a guilt she wanted to relieve herself of. Lady Green's conscience controlled the expression on her face, and Gladys saw the eyes of a woman wracked with shame.

"Well?" said Gladys. "Can we come in, or am I going to take this letter to the police, and I don't mean Inspector Jameson."

Hearing the name of the man who was somehow implicit in the cover-up was the final motivation Lady Green required. She stood aside and slowly opened the door wider. "You'd better come in," she murmured.

CHAPTER FIFTEEN

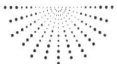

The house had nothing on Huang Towers, but it was impressive nonetheless. Large oil paintings hung on the wood panelled walls, and antique furniture added to the home's regal appearance.

Lady Green led them to a large room with tall windows which overlooked the grounds, and enough seating to host a large gathering of people. Gladys took a seat on a creaky Chesterfield sofa, and Penny and Willow sat alongside her, one on either side.

"I suppose you'd all like a drink?" said Lady Green, opening a hardwood drinks cabinet, complete with a small freezer compartment built into it. "I know I do."

Penny and Willow declined the offer, but Gladys never turned down a free drink, especially from a cabinet on top of which were placed cut-crystal glasses. "A sherry, please," she said. "Not too large, and not too small."

Lady Green prepared the drinks with the practised skill of somebody who was no stranger to alcohol, adding a single ice-cube to her whisky, and tucking the bottle under her arm. She handed Gladys her sherry, and sat down opposite the three witches in a large armchair, looking at them in turn. She placed the bottle on a small table next to the chair. "I recognise you three," she said. "I keep a low profile in town, but I've seen you around over the years." She concentrated on Penny. "You own a boat don't you? And you run that little magic shop with your sister."

Gladys sipped her sherry, being sure to extend her little finger, but bringing it quickly back into line. Was that delicate social manoeuvre reserved only for the taking of tea? Or was it apt for alcohol too? She'd have to find out before she hosted another party in Huang Towers. She didn't want to look silly. Lady Green hadn't extended her finger, in fact, she was throwing whisky down her neck with the enthusiasm of a sailor on shore-leave.

"Yes, that's right," said Penny. "We run the shop."

"There's no time for small talk, Lady Green," said

Gladys. "Let's get straight to the nitty-gritty. What happened all those years ago?"

"I think you should go first," said Lady Green. "How do you know anything about what happened, and how did you get that letter? Did Ethel give it to you? That woman should know better. She's under an oath."

Gladys chose her words carefully. Ethel was dead, but Lady Green didn't know that. "We think Ethel may be in danger," she said. "We know your son was recently released from prison — and we know he was imprisoned on a fake charge implemented by your husband and the police. We're worried he may want to cause trouble for Ethel."

Lady Green poured herself more whisky. "Does Inspector Jameson know you're here? He's always looked out for Ethel. If he had any concerns, he'd have come and seen me himself. When I gave him that letter for Ethel, he told me nobody knew where my son had gone when he was released from prison. I don't understand why you three are here and not the inspector."

"Lady Green," said Willow, leaning forward and brushing the hair from her eyes. "What happened to Ethel Boyd in the chapel? Tell us."

Lady Green took a long swallow of whisky and

gave a drawn out sigh. "I suppose it's time to get it off my chest," she said. "It's been burning a hole in my heart for all these years — what happened to Ethel, and what we did to my son. What my *husband* did to my son. I didn't want any part in a cover-up. I wanted it all out in the open, but back then, reputations were everything."

Gladys wondered if Willow had cast a truth spell, but as Lady Green drank more whisky, Gladys realised she was under the spell of the oldest truth potion known to mankind. Alcohol. "Tell us everything," said Gladys. "From the beginning. You'll feel better afterwards."

Lady Green held her glass up, allowing the light streaming from the window to illuminate the amber liquid. "It began with this," she said, swirling the whisky in her glass.

"Whisky?" said Penny.

"Alcohol," said Lady Green. "I was always partial to a drop, and it seems like I passed my genes on to my son. Not my youngest son, he doesn't touch it, but my eldest son — the one you're talking about. Rupert. He liked it a little too much."

Gladys sipped her sherry. "Where are your other children?" she said. "It says in your letter to Ethel that you're surrounded by them."

"A lie," said Lady Green, the words flowing freer with each sip of whisky she took. "I don't want her to know how alone I am. My children stopped visiting us years ago. When they found out what we'd done to Rupert."

"What did you do?" said Willow.

Lady Green gazed at her glass, her eyes glazed. "Rupert was such a good boy until he discovered alcohol, then he went off the rails. Him and a group of boys in town, always drunk and always getting into trouble. My husband and I put it down to teenagers being teenagers, but when the other boys went off to university and began building their lives, it became apparent that Rupert was more dependant on alcohol than we'd ever imagined. A little like me."

"How sad," said Penny.

"It *was* sad," said Lady Green. "It was heartbreaking. But when he was caught drink driving, it became too much. My husband was an important man, not only was he a Lord, but he was a judge too. He had a reputation to protect. Benjamin spoke to the police superintendent and the charges were dropped. That was the first time he used his privileged position to influence the law."

"But not the last," said Gladys.

Lady Green shook her head. "No. When the

charges of drink driving were dropped, my husband pulled some more strings. Rupert had no university degree, but Benjamin knew a lot of people who were high up in the church. We arranged to send him off to train as a vicar.

" It worked, and Rupert stopped drinking for years. Although his position as a vicar had been manipulated by my husband, Rupert began to enjoy it, and my husband and I were overjoyed. We were both very religious people deep down, and the little chapel near the canal was on our land.

"Rupert took it over and built up quite a congregation. He began to see the chapel as his rock— a place to find comfort in. He became very highly respected, and nobody was any wiser about his previous problems with alcohol. We were proud of him."

"Proud…" said Gladys. She'd seen enough detective shows on TV to know that you didn't let somebody stop talking when they'd started. You needed to keep grinding their gears. "…until nineteen-eighty-seven."

"Yes," said Lady Green, fiddling with her necklace. "That was an awful year. Rupert began drinking again, you see. He had a terrible problem, and his father and I decided to cut him off from money. He wasn't getting paid to be a vicar. Like I said, his *posi-*

tion was manipulated by my husband and some people in the church. The only money Rupert was getting was from me and his father, and when he started drinking it away, we cut him off completely. We fed and clothed him, of course, but we wouldn't pay to feed his habit. It was hypocritical of me, as a drinker myself, but I was nothing like Rupert. He didn't know when to stop."

"Go on," said Gladys.

"Well, he found a creative way of obtaining money. He began a collection every Sunday. Him and Ethel Boyd would hand a plate around, and the good people of the congregation would fill it with money."

"Which went on booze," said Penny.

Lady Green sighed. "Yes. He stole the money and spent it on alcohol. Drugs too. He was a mess. He'd hide in his little cave, drinking, taking drugs, and wasting his life."

"Cave?" said Gladys.

"Underneath the chapel," said Lady Green. "That's why it was called cave chapel. There are caves everywhere in the hills around Wickford, and the man who first built the chapel was as dishonest a vicar as my son was. He built it over the cave, and so close to the canal, to advance his business in stealing from haulage boats.

"He had arrangements with a lot of the narrowboat crews. They'd sell him a portion of the coal, or whatever load they were carrying, and the vicar would hide it beneath the chapel. Nobody would have thought a little chapel was built above a storage facility for stolen goods, so he got away with it — selling it on, and lining his pockets. The entrance is hidden behind the chapel, so not even his congregation knew it was there."

"You're getting off track," said Willow. "What happened between your son and Ethel?"

Lady Green may have gone off on a tangent, but something she had said was worming its way through Gladys's mind. She couldn't quite put her finger on what it was, or why it may have been important, but it was there — like a distant voice on the wind.

"As I said," continued Lady Green. "He sat in that little cave, drinking and taking drugs — all from the proceeds of dishonesty. We didn't know of course, or we'd have put a stop to it. We only found out afterwards, when Ethel told us. When she could speak again."

"Speak again?" said Gladys. "What do you mean?"

"It was awful," said Lady Green with a shudder. "Rupert took a liking to Ethel... in *that* way. She wasn't like the other people in the congregation. *They'd* all come to church in their Sunday best, but Ethel would come in a snazzy shell-suit. She said it was more comfortable to play the organ in, but I know she was wearing it to turn Rupert's head."

"They were in love?" said Willow.

"Oh gosh, no," said Lady Green. "It didn't get that far. At least from Ethel's perspective. Rupert made the mistake of thinking he could trust Ethel. Ethel may have had her eye on being a vicar's wife but, she wasn't dishonest. One morning, on a Wednesday, Ethel went to the chapel to practice on the organ. Rupert was drinking in his cave of delinquency, and when he heard Ethel playing he came up to see her.

"He was drunk — he wasn't thinking straight, and he boasted to Ethel about how he was stealing the money and spending it on drink and drugs. He showed Ethel the cave, and Ethel did the right thing by God, but not by Rupert."

"What did she do?" said Willow.

"She told him she was going to report him to the police," said Lady Green, a tear swelling in her eye. "She should have come to us, but no, she threatened him with the law, and it scared him. He was so drunk and high on drugs that he wasn't thinking straight."

"What did he do?" said Gladys.

Lady Green let out a sob. "Ethel went back into the chapel to collect her sheet music, and as she was sitting at the organ, Rupert came up behind her and hit her over the head with a full bottle of vodka."

"Oh, my," said Gladys. "What an awful man."

"Yes," said Lady Green, "but something, or someone, spoke to him, and guided him back onto the correct path. The honest path. He came straight here, to this house, and told me what he'd done. I phoned the police of course, and Rupert ran off, back to the chapel. When Benjamin heard what had happened, he was furious with me for phoning the police, and by the time the police got to the chapel, the cover-up had begun.

"Benjamin knew a lot of powerful people — people in government, people he'd known since his Oxford days. The phone calls were made quickly, people's jobs were threatened, and the incident was never reported. If Ethel had died, I think it would have been different, but the hospital said she'd come out of the coma within a few days. Which she did."

"Wow," said Willow. "The poor woman."

"Yes," said Lady Green. "The poor woman. Benjamin and I didn't know what to do with Rupert. He was a drug addicted alcoholic man who'd nearly killed a woman. We were ashamed, and Benjamin had his reputation to think of. Rupert had to be taught a lesson, although I think we went too far."

"You had him locked away for murder," said Gladys. "Which he was innocent of."

"By sheer luck," said Lady Green. "Ethel was close to death, so we told Rupert she'd died, and Benjamin set up a mock trial using every favour he was owed by some of the most important people in the land. The jury was real, and the judge was real — a friend of Benjamin's, but everything else was manufactured. The evidence, the pathologists report, everything. When the the jury found him guilty, the judge sentenced him to thirty years, and he was never told that Ethel didn't die. He still thinks he's a murderer."

"And you bribed Ethel and Inspector Jameson?" said Penny.

"We offered Ethel money, yes, and she accepted it, but Inspector Jameson didn't. He only did what Ethel asked him to do. He's a good man," said Lady Green. "My husband was a hard man. I had no control over his decisions, and things were different all those years ago. There was more corruption, and when a reporter began poking his nose where Benjamin didn't want it, he was sent to prison too, on a fake drugs charge."

The reporter who Susie had spoken to, realised

Gladys. She closed her eyes for a moment, the flavour of sherry still warming her throat, and her mind working towards something — slowly, but surely.

Gladys knew she wasn't a clever woman, not in the academic sense, but she did know that her mind was keen. Not quite as keen as mustard, but keen enough.

She liked to think of her mind as a kitchen cutlery draw, with the utensils she used regularly near the front — easily accessible and ready for use. At the back of the drawer, in a messy pile, were the things that she collected, but used infrequently — like the hard boiled egg slicer, and the little melon baller that Eva had bought her for Christmas.

It was there — at the back of the drawer, tucked away in the darkest recesses of her mind, that she found them — the little jumble of thoughts which had turned into an idea. No — it was more than an idea — it was an answer. *The* answer. The answer to the question of who had killed Ethel Boyd.

She stood up. "Penny, Willow," she said. "We need to leave."

CHAPTER SIXTEEN

Gladys's knee creaked as she lowered herself behind the bush, and she snapped her head to the right as Barney's radio crackled into life. "Turn that off!" she hissed. "We have to be quiet. This is a stake-out!"

Barney twisted the knob on his radio and it fell silent. "Are you sure about this, Gladys?" he said. "You haven't told us how you've come to this conclusion."

Gladys tapped the side of her head with a finger. "It's all up here, sunshine," she said. "I'll explain how I worked it out in due course."

A branch snapped as Willow adjusted her position, and Gladys scowled at her. "Would you keep silent, please?"

"Are you sure he'll come?" said Penny.

Gladys peeped through the bush. The rear of the chapel was twenty metres to their front, and a pathway led off into the woods to the right. "If Barney did his job properly he should be here shortly."

"Of course I did," said Barney. "I found him near the butcher's shop, and told him he had to move on. He headed out of town, I watched him and then came straight here."

Gladys nodded. "Just you wait," she said. "With no more spells preventing people approaching the chapel, we should have a visitor in the very near future."

Gladys steadied her breathing. She was about to confront Ethel's murderer, and she wanted to be calm when she did so. There could be no room for emotion in a highly charged situation such as the one she was in.

She allowed her knees to sink further into the pine needles, and kept her eyes on the pathway. She revelled in the excitement, her heart thudding on her chest wall, and her stomach in anxious knots.

Time ticked by, and after thirty minutes of waiting, even Gladys had become restless. She stood up slowly, allowing her knees time to recover, and joined the other three as they plucked blackberries from a nearby bush. They tasted good, and Gladys stuffed her mouth with the sweet fruit, wiping the juice from her chin with the back of her hand. As she chewed, she realised she had a new found respect for the police. She didn't know how they managed to stay so still on stake-outs, for hours on end. She span on the spot. "Did you hear that?" she said.

"What? Said Penny.

"A man shouting," said Gladys, cupping a hand behind her ear.

They stood still, listening, and just as Gladys was about to get back to fruit picking, she heard it again, this time closer, and clearer. "Bonnie!" came the man's voice. "Bonnie! Where are you?"

Gladys sank to her knees and urged the others to join her.

"Who's Bonnie?" whispered Willow.

"Not *who*," said Gladys. "*What.*"

A blur of white streaked through the clearing to their front, followed by the sound of exciting barking.

"That's Bonnie," said Gladys. "The little terrier that Mavis saw."

"How did you know its name?" said Penny.

"I didn't," said Gladys, "but I guessed it belonged to the murderer."

The man shouted again, now much closer, and

with excitement in his voice. "Bonnie! There you are! I'm so sorry, girl! I couldn't find my way back to you. I kept getting lost! But I'm here now, and I've got something special for you."

He hadn't been lost, just confused by a spell, but Gladys could never tell him that. She could show off and tell the other three what the man had brought for his dog, though. "Scraps of kidney and liver," she whispered. "Just you watch."

A branch snapped to their front, and Gladys lowered herself even closer to the ground. "Quiet," she hissed. "He's here."

Branches parted, and the little dog scampered into the clearing followed by its owner, who staggered behind it, clutching a paper bag in one hand, and a bottle of vodka in the other.

"The homeless man you told us about," whispered Penny.

Gladys smiled. "Let me introduce you to Rupert Green, shamed vicar of Cave Chapel, and Ethel Boyd's murderer."

Barney reached for his night-stick, and Gladys put a hand on his arm. "No, Barney," she said. "I worked it out, I want to confront him. I've got a little speech planned and everything!"

Barney nodded. "We'll all go together, but you

can speak to him. If he tries anything funny, I'm right here."

"So are we," said Willow. "There are three witches here, Barney. I'm sure we'll be fine."

Barney took his hand off his night-stick. "Watch out for the dog, those terriers are snappy little things."

"Just wait," said Gladys. "He's going to show us where the entrance to the cave beneath the chapel is, and when he goes inside, we'll follow him. He'll be trapped."

The little dog jumped up at its owner as the two of them headed for the chapel. The man who Gladys assumed was Rupert Green, squeezed through a gap in the fence railings and made the sign of the cross on his chest.

He pushed through the long grass and made his way to the rear of the chapel, where he bent over and parted the large bushes which grew against the wall.

"No wonder you couldn't find it," said Barney. "It's overgrown."

Gladys and the girls had made a cursory search for the entrance while Barney was in town looking for the man, but had failed to find any sign of it.

"I'd have found it eventually," said Gladys. "We didn't have much time, that was all."

Gladys watched as the man fumbled with something at his feet. A creaking sound gave away the fact he'd opened a door of some kind, and he stood up and beckoned his dog. "Come on, Bonnie. It's time for me to have a drink, and for you to have some kidneys and liver," he said.

He disappeared into the ground, his movement suggesting he was descending stairs, and his dog followed, letting out an excited yap. The door creaked again as he closed it behind himself, and the clearing fell silent.

"Told you," said Gladys. "Kidneys and liver." She felt a rush of guilt. She hoped the dog had been okay while its master had not been able to find his way back to the chapel. It looked healthy enough, and with numerous farms dotted around the area and boats moored along the canal, Gladys was sure it would have found food.

She stood up, her knee aching. It was nice being in Wickford, but she missed the health benefits of The Haven. She'd forgotten how many aches and twinges of pain she'd suffered from before making her home in Huang Towers, her health bolstered by magic. "Let's go," she said. "Follow me, and let *me* do the talking. I've already spoken with him, we've got a bond, plus — I've got a way with words that none of you have."

Gladys led the way towards the chapel, wincing as her knee spasmed in pain. She used the same gap in the rails that Rupert had used, and waited as the others squeezed through the fence behind her. She moved slowly through the grass, pausing as she reached the bushes that grew tight alongside the chapel wall. "No wonder we couldn't find it," she said, parting the foliage. "It's completely hidden."

The only sign of an entrance were the iron hinges and a raised concrete lip. The rest of the entrance was disguised by thick ivy and moss. Two metal handles jutted from the centre of the doorway, and Gladys realised it was a entrance much the same as the ones that pubs used to fill their cellars with fresh barrels of beer. She grabbed one of the handles, and gave it a tug. "It's stuck," she said. "Or very heavy. Rupert must be stronger than the average drunk."

Barney stepped past Gladys. "Let me open it," he said.

Gladys wiggled her fingers. "I can manage."

"No, not with magic," said Barney. "I suspect the spell you'd use to open a heavy wooden door would be as subtle as a SWAT team kicking the door in. We don't want to alarm him — frightened people don't react well."

"Quickly then," said Gladys. "I want this over

with. I need him in custody and I need my chapel back to normal ASAP."

Barney grabbed a handle with both hands and pulled. A vein in his neck bulged angrily beneath his skin as he straightened his back, but the door moved — slowly at first, the musty stench of damp greeting their noses as the entrance widened. Barney lifted it to an almost upright position, and held it in place. "The hinges have rusted," he whispered. "This is as far as it will open. You three will have to hold it, and I'll go in."

"Nonsense," said Gladys. "I'm going first. It's my chapel, and I've got magic to protect myself with. You follow me, Barney. The girls can hold the door open for us."

"No," hissed Barney. "Let me go in."

Gladys ignored him. She stepped into the hole and peered down the steps. Orange light danced over the rock walls of the staircase, the flickering of the light suggesting the source was a flame. She placed her foot carefully on the next step and lowered her head to avoid the low ceiling as she began to descend. The rock hewn steps were home to a layer of damp moss, and Gladys placed her feet carefully, the soles of her shoes struggling to find purchase on the ice-like surface.

Gladys sniffed the air. Kerosene. She was familiar with the smell — it was the same sweet aroma which had filled her tomato glasshouse on winter nights, when a heater was required to save the plants from frost damage. She looked up at Barney, who was preparing to follow her. "Be careful," she whispered. "The steps are slippery."

Gladys dropped her eyes back to the steps, and gave a frightened gasp. She instinctively tried to move backwards — away from the looming shape of a man which came at her with speed, but the combination of slippery steps and her aching knee was too much. Both feet flew from beneath her, and she prepared herself for the fall which she knew was coming. With no time to even think of a spell, let alone cast one, Gladys tried to relax her body as much as possible, hoping that looser muscles would cause less pain when they collided with rock.

Time slowed in her mind, and Gladys was aware that the man was pushing past her, breaking her fall a little, but reaching for the door which Barney still held open.

Gladys heard the door slam shut, and she heard Barney shouting, but as her body thudded into the steps, the base of her back taking the brunt of the force and winding her, she heard the tell-tale sound of a locking bolt sliding into place.

As her head slammed into the hard cave floor, and the sound of a dog's frantic barking bounced off the walls, Gladys realised that not only was she hurt, but she was trapped in a cave — with a man who was quite capable of violence.

She concentrated on the ball in her chest, attempting to take control of her magic, but without being able to take proper breaths, she didn't have the ability. Her vision wobbled, and her back hurt, and as footsteps descended the stairs behind her, she swallowed.

She was at Rupert Green's mercy. She closed her eyes and regretted not allowing Barney to enter the cave before her.

CHAPTER SEVENTEEN

Gladys opened her eyes. It was hard to see — not because of the dim lighting, but because her glasses were no longer perched on her nose. She attempted to get to her feet, the floor damp and cold beneath her hands, but a large booted foot pressed down hard on her wrist, making her gasp as her bones met unforgiving rock.

The thuds on the door, and the frantic shouts of Barney and her granddaughters, told Gladys that they were attempting to get to her, but the door was thick, and she doubted the man who'd built the chapel to hide stolen goods beneath had skimped on the quality of the lock. Penny or Willow would open it with magic eventually, but the stress they must be under would make it harder for them to find the appropriate spell and make it work correctly. She needed to buy time.

"Rupert," said Gladys, her ribs stinging as she spoke. "I only came here to talk to you."

"What are you?" shouted Rupert, bending over Gladys. "I knew there was something about you when you were bothering me in town. What are you? A ghost like the one upstairs, in the chapel?" He moved his face closer to hers. "No – you're worse than that, you're a vampire aren't you? Look at the blood on your face — you've fed recently, haven't you? You've sucked the blood from some poor soul and cast their drained carcass aside like an empty cider can! Well, you won't be feeding on me!"

"What are you talking about?" said Gladys. "I'm not a vampire!" Realisation dawned on her. "It's blackberry juice! The stuff on my lips and chin! I was eating blackberries! It's not blood!"

Rupert took a step away from her. "Quiet, Bonnie!" he snapped at the little dog. "Let me get the lantern, we'll have a proper look at her."

The little dog stopped barking, and Gladys's cheek warmed as the little animal sniffed at her face, its breath hot and its nose wet.

Gladys searched the floor around her, using both hands to feel for her glasses. Puddles of moisture cooled her hands as her fingertips crisscrossed the hard floor, and she ignored the pain in her ribs as she forced her arms further from her body. Bonnie sniffed at Gladys's hand as she dragged it in a search arc around her body, and then she felt it — one of the welcoming plastic arms of her cheap spectacles.

Rupert's footsteps approached, and the dancing lights on the walls grew brighter. Gladys fumbled with her glasses, managing to get them on her face just as Rupert swung the lantern over her and bent down to study her face.

With her eyes fully functional, Gladys's fear intensified. She was looking into the face of a man who couldn't be bargained with. He was too high on drugs or drink to listen to reason, and Gladys hoped that Barney and the girls would be able to open the door soon. The thuds on the wood had become desperate, and Gladys could hear the stress in Penny and Willow's voices as they shouted. The girls needed to calm down — Gladys could feel *her* control over magic slowly returning, but the girls would find it hard to cast a spell if they remained so panicked.

"Hmmm," said Rupert, the alcohol on his acrid breath flooding Gladys's nostrils. "It's not blood after all. Maybe you're not a vampire, but there's something about you that I don't like. I can't risk keeping you alive, not with those other people, or *things,* trying to get into my cave. Maybe they'll go away when their queen is dead."

"You're mad," said Gladys. "I just came here to talk to you, Rupert. You have to open the door — there's a policeman outside."

Rupert's face twisted with rage and his pupils darkened. The light cast by the lantern picked out the hard edges of his face, and his words came in a guttural roar. "I am not mad!" he shouted, flecks of his spittle wetting Gladys's face. "Don't call me mad!" Rupert balled his free hand into a fist, the bandage draped around it filthy and tattered, and took aim at Gladys's face, a foot on either side of her prone body, and the lantern swinging erratically in his other hand.

"No!' shouted Gladys, her magic refusing to cooperate, and her blood running cold as fear took its grip on her.

Rupert was beyond listening to an elderly woman's pleas, and as his fist began the journey towards Gladys's face, she knew she must act.

The way to a man's heart was through his stomach — Gladys was fully onboard with that concept, but it wasn't Rupert's heart she wanted to reach — it was the pain receptors in his brain, and the target which would allow her to access to those, was a few inches lower than his stomach.

Gladys brought her foot up with as much force as she could muster, ignoring the pain in her back, and aiming the hard toe of her shoe at the soft baggage hidden by Rupert's trousers.

Rupert's fist closed in on Gladys quickly, and as her foot made contact with its target, she slid her head to the side. The sound which Rupert made was more of a squeal than a yell of pain, and Gladys wondered if he'd even felt his fist slam into the cave floor next to her head. He bent at the waist and fell to the ground, both hands instinctively reaching for his groin, the lantern clattering to the floor next to him, the glass breaking and releasing a river of kerosene fuelled flames.

Bonnie yelped as flames spread across the floor, and Gladys moved her leg as the heat brushed the outside of her ankle. The flowing stream of fire rushed towards Rupert, and he screamed louder as his trousers began to melt, the cheap material igniting immediately, the flames quickly working their way along his writhing legs.

Gladys knew what it was like to be burned to death, and the flames scared her, she wasn't afraid to admit it. There was no way she was going to allow a fellow human to endure the pain she'd suffered, though. *No way*. Whatever he'd done, Rupert did not deserve to feel the very blood in his veins boiling as he struggled to hold onto life.

Gladys dug deep for her magic, aware that the banging on the door was getting louder, and that Bonnie was running in frightened circles as the flaming pool of kerosene spread across the cave floor. She coughed as smoke filled her airways, but composed herself enough to be able to close her eyes and focus on her magical essence.

The ball in her chest grew hotter as flames warmed the air around her, and Gladys took a deep breath, her mind's eye already picturing the spell she wanted to cast. She imagined ice-bergs, and she imagined glaciers, and as the magic ran through her limbs, her fingertips ejected ice-blue sparks of pure energy.

Gladys took a final breath and cast her spell, the sparks at her fingertips transforming into a cold blast of freezing magic which twisted in the air, searching out heat, wrapping it in cold and smothering it wherever it was found.

When the flames were smothered, Gladys used another spell, a spell which hovered above her head, casting the cave in an amber light.

Rupert moaned and groaned, his legs a mess of

burnt flesh and globules of melted polyester. Bonnie licked her master's face, her whines of fear breaking Gladys's heart. The cave was large, spanning almost the full length of the chapel above it, but it was fast becoming too smoke clogged to allow normal breathing. Even with no fire, smoke continued to rise.

Gladys coughed, and mustered her energy again. Her pain could wait. Now the flames were extinguished, Rupert required a healing spell before she did, and she couldn't bear to watch the little dog so anxious about her owner's health. Rupert's welfare had to come first.

The spell came easily, and Rupert's groans became gentle whimpers as his flesh knitted itself together, expelling the fragments of material from the charred blisters as they grew new skin and hair. She made sure to leave the wound she guessed was beneath the bandage on his hand intact. She suspected it was evidence, and healing it would not help her case.

A crashing sound behind her made her jump, and Bonnie gave a warning bark as the broken door smashed into the steps, the residual sparks of magic in the air giving away the fact that magic had broken through the thick wood, and not brute force.

"Granny!" shouted Penny, taking the steps in two long bounds, her feet slipping on the moss. "Granny!"

Gladys cast a healing spell over her body, sighing as the agonising pain in her ribs and back ceased, replaced with the welcome warmth of fresh vigour. "I'm okay, dear," she said. "We should get Rupert and Bonnie out of here, though. They both need fresh air."

"What happened?" said Barney, his night-stick in his hand and his brow furrowed with deep concern.

"Did he hurt you?" said Willow.

Gladys held out a hand. "Help me up. Let's get Rupert into the chapel and wake him up. I didn't get around to speaking to him about Ethel after all. There are still a lot of questions that need an answer."

CHAPTER EIGHTEEN

"How did you know he was Rupert Green, Granny?" said Willow, staring at the half conscious groaning man.

Barney had propped him up on a pew, and his wrists were secured with handcuffs. Gladys had cast a spell over his trousers, repairing them, and nobody would have been any the wiser about the fact that he'd almost met his death in a fire.

Bonnie eagerly lapped at the water which Willow had collected from the canal, and Gladys had brought the paper bag of liver and kidneys from the cave. The dog seemed unharmed by its ordeal, and Gladys had already decided she was going to take it back to The Haven with her. Living in a cave with a drunkard was no life for the little dog, especially a drunkard who was soon to be in prison.

Ethel's body remained in position at the organ, but Barney had covered it with a sheet from his police car. Her body remained in stasis, and when Gladys finally released her body from the spell, no pathologist in the land would be able to tell that the woman had been dead for days and not minutes or hours.

Gladys clasped her hands behind her back. *It was her moment*. Her moment to shine. She began pacing — walking left and right as she studied the man in handcuffs. "A few things dropped into place when we visited Lady Green," she explained, answering Willow's question. "When I first met Rupert, he introduced himself as The Bear— a name that meant nothing to me until Lady Green informed us of her son's name. I quickly deduced it was a nickname foisted upon him by his fellow lags in prison — a crude reference to his name — Rupert."

"Are you pretending to be a TV detective again, Gladys?" said Barney. "Because if you are, you're wasting time. Just give us the facts."

Gladys ignored him. She had plenty of time. When Gladys had finished presenting her case, she was going to ask Barney to report the discovery of Ethel's body. With the murderer present at the scene it wouldn't take long until all evidence had been collected and Ethel's body had been removed.

Gladys had plenty of time to wrap the case up in the style she'd imagined herself doing it in. She continued pacing. "Of course, there was more to it than that. A simple name wouldn't have allowed me to break this case open like a particularly tough brazil nut. No, I needed to fit the pieces together — like a flat packed table, if you will."

"Or a jigsaw puzzle?" suggested Penny.

Gladys sighed. "A jigsaw has a picture on the box. You know the answer before you even begin the puzzle. A flat packed table has instructions written in Chinglish, and diagrams which appear to be drawn by a blind fellow with no experience of DIY. My analogy stands!"

"Okay, Granny," said Willow, "we're listening."

"When I first met Rupert," continued Gladys, peering at the prisoner over her spectacles, "I told him to crawl back under his stone. His answer puzzled me. He replied that it wasn't a stone — it was more of a rock. To the casual observer that may have come across as a boast, but with my keen mind I was able to see past his throwaway statement. My suspicions were first aroused when Brian mentioned that Ethel called the chapel her rock — as in *a place of solace.* When Lady Green used the same terminology to describe how Rupert had thought of the chapel, the pieces slipped into place like a well oiled… mechanism of some description."

"Machine?" said Barney. "A well oiled machine?"

"Precisely," said Gladys. "You'll go far, Barney. Add into the mix that Rupert complained he couldn't find his way home — not a reference to how drunk or disorientated he was, but a tantalising clue that perhaps my spell was keeping him away from his home. Of course, none of it made sense until Lady Green informed us about the cave beneath the chapel, but I'd have got there eventually. The wheels in my brain were already in full forward motion."

Barney stepped forward and stared at Rupert Green. "So we know he's —"

"I haven't finished!" said Gladys. "I'll have no more interruptions, thank you very much!" She paced slowly, making her way towards one of the broken chapel windows. "When Lady Green informed us that her son had been a man of God, I immediately recalled him making the sign of the cross when I met him for the second time. Of course, it's mostly catholics who make that sign, but Rupert's rise to vicardom was manipulated. He knew no different. He was an ill-trained man of the church."

Gladys paused, and peered at her audience. "The

final piece of the puzzle was the fact I'd seen the butcher hand over a bag of meat scraps to Rupert. A meal fit for a man? Possibly, but unlikely — even for a man down on his luck. When I recalled that Mavis had seen a little white dog on the day of Ethel's death, I came to my conclusion — the homeless man I'd seen in town was Rupert Green, and he was living in the cave he'd once found drunken solace in. Lady Green tied it all together for me, but the pieces were there in my mind, and I take full credit for solving the murder of Ethel Boyd."

"But how and why did he kill Ethel?" said Willow. "If he did, of course."

"Of course he did," said Gladys. "We'll ask him *why* when we wake him up, but as to *how* he killed her — Barney would you be so kind as to take that filthy bandage off Rupert Green's hand, please?"

Barney did as Gladys asked. When he'd unravelled the dirty length of fabric and placed it on the pew next to Rupert, Gladys smiled. "Tell us what you see, Barney."

Barney inspected Rupert's hand. "A gash,' he said. "A deep one, on his palm."

Gladys smiled. She bent over and picked up a sliver of broken glass that had fallen from the smashed window behind her. "Made by stained glass!" she announced, holding the glass aloft. "When the forensics people get here, Barney, you can bet they'll find glass in Ethel's wound, and probably in the gash in Rupert's hand too. The murder weapon was never a knife."

Willow cleared her throat and smiled. "So it literally was Reverend Green, in the chapel, with —"

"No!" shouted Gladys. She felt her breath leave her in a gasp of frustration. That had been *her* punchline — the moment she'd been working towards since Lady Green had provided the information Gladys had required to solve the crime.

She steadied herself and took a calming breath. "No! That's not right, Willow. Not right at all!" she said. "Rupert was a vicar, not a reverend! It doesn't work, darling. I'm sorry, but if you want to make wisecracks, please make sure they work. Not forgetting of course, that Ethel's body is still in the room — do you think she wants to hear you making light of her death?"

"No, Granny," said Willow, twisting her toe into the floor. "I'm sorry."

"Good. Now let's not here another word about it," said Gladys, making her way towards Rupert. "It's time to wake him up. The sleeping spell I added to the healing spell is weak. It'll be simple to rouse him."

"W<small>AKE UP</small>, R<small>UPERT</small>," said Gladys, splashing some water on the man's face.

"What the?" moaned Rupert, his eyes adjusting to his surroundings. "How did I get here? The last thing I remember was opening my bottle of vodka." He struggled against the metal binding his wrists. "Why am I in handcuffs?"

Gladys wasted no time. She pointed at the organ. With the sheet removed, Ethel's body made a harrowing sight. "Why did you kill her, Rupert?"

Rupert stared at Ethel. "A ghost," he said. "I killed a ghost. She came here to haunt me — for what I'd done to her all those years ago, but I've already been punished. They put me in prison. Why does she still want to torment me? She's even wearing the same shell-suit she was wearing when I killed her, and she's brought a ghost organ with her. Why are ghosts so cruel?"

Gladys's stomach tightened, and despair washed over her. She hadn't expected Rupert to admit to his crime immediately, but when he *had* confessed, she'd expected him to have spoken about the killing being his revenge for the time he'd spent in prison. Gladys had assumed that Rupert had found out he'd spent thirty years in prison for a murder he hadn't committed. The truth was more harrowing.

Gladys looked at Ethel's body. With her hair dyed, and wearing the same shell-suit she'd worn when Rupert had attacked her thirty years ago, Ethel could have been any age when viewed from behind. Gladys recalled Ethel telling her the shell-suit made her feel safe. *It hadn't worked*. She stared at Rupert. "You think she's a ghost?" said Gladys.

"Of course she is," said Rupert, straining at the cuffs. "I killed her thirty years ago, and her ghost was waiting for me when I came back. I'd only been back in Wickford for a few days. I came here to find Ethel's grave. I wanted to say sorry, but I couldn't find her in any of the cemeteries.

"I didn't know what to do — I had nowhere to live, and not much money — my parents had told me I was never welcome at home again, so I came straight here, to see if my old chapel was still standing. When I found it was, I moved into the cave. There was a little stray dog living along the canal bank, and when I took her in, I had everything I needed — somewhere to stay dry, and a loyal friend to share my home with."

"What happened?" said Gladys. "Why did you kill Ethel… Ethel's ghost?"

Rupert attempted to move his hands. "Why am I in handcuffs? What are you accusing me of? Yes, I take drugs, and yes, I drink too much, but I'm not a criminal. Not anymore. I did my time! I paid my penance!"

"Calm down," said Barney, asserting his policeman's authority. "Answer the question, Rupert. "What happened here? What happened with you and the… ghost?"

Rupert licked his lips, his tongue wetting the thick strands of hair which made up his beard. "I was in my cave," he said. "Drunk and high. Bonnie woke me up, she was barking, I think. I can't remember. It's all muddled."

"Try to remember," said Gladys. "What happened when you woke up?"

Rupert looked at the ceiling. "I… I heard the music. Yes, that's right. I heard the organ being played in the chapel, but I knew there was no organ in the chapel — I'd already looked around. I was spooked."

"So you came up here?" urged Gladys. "To have a look?"

Rupert nodded. "Yes, and then I saw it. At the impossible organ." Rupert shuddered. "I couldn't believe my eyes. I've always been fascinated with stories about ghosts and vampires, but when I saw one in real life, I was terrified. I shouted, but it didn't hear me — it was playing the organ too loud. My vision was blurred, you know how it is when you're high?"

Gladys nodded.

"So I moved closer," said Rupert, "and I picked up a weapon. A piece of glass. Then I saw it. The beautiful clothing, the same lovely clothing that Ethel had been wearing on the day I committed my wicked crime. It was her! It was her ghost! I didn't know what to do. I loved Ethel, but it wasn't Ethel siting at the organ — it was something else, something not of this world, something that had no place in the chapel.

"I wasn't sure what to do, and then I remembered the stories I'd read — ghosts wander the earth until they can finally pass over. So I stabbed it, in the back of the neck, with the glass. I cut myself too. So deep it didn't bleed, but I didn't worry about that. I'd killed the ghost! And I'd set Ethel's spirit free. Free to move on to the next world!"

Gladys sighed. It was a tragic tale. "What did you do after you'd killed it?"

"It kept playing the organ," said Rupert. "One continuous note. It was terrifying, so I ran away. Into town. To get more drink and drugs. Bonnie ran in the other direction, as scared by the sound as I was. I waited around for a few hours, and when I tried to get back here, I couldn't find the chapel. I kept wandering in circles until I ended up back in town."

The spell to keep people away had worked well, but Gladys had no stomach for congratulating herself on her magical prowess. She was embroiled in an ethical dilemma. A dilemma so sad she could have shed a tear. Rupert had spent thirty years in prison for a murder he hadn't committed. Yes, he'd attacked and severely hurt Ethel, but the time he'd spent in prison because of a cover up was hard for Gladys to consider fair. Rupert had wandered into a chapel where a woman he'd already killed was playing an organ that shouldn't have been there, and he'd been in the grip of a drugs and alcohol stupor. It had been a tragedy.

"Can you take the handcuffs off, please?' said Rupert. "I know my rights, and I need a fix. I've got cold sweats, and my head hurts!"

Gladys looked at Barney. "Call it in," she said. "Tell them we came here so Ethel could practice on the organ. We'll tell them what really did happen — we stepped outside, to see if we could hear the organ from the canal. We heard Ethel playing one terrible note, and when we came back, she was dead. We'll tell them Bonnie was frantic, and she led us to the cave where we found Rupert. He'll admit what he did, and all the evidence is here. They'll have it wrapped up in no time."

"The wound on his hand is days old, though," said Willow. "Somebody will notice it wasn't made today."

Gladys glanced at Rupert. She didn't want to hurt him, but she'd add a painkiller to the spell which would freshen up the gash on his hand.

Rupert winced as Gladys took his hand in hers and applied the spell. The edges of the wound softened, and the infection began to heal. She felt less guilt for meddling with his wound —she'd done him a favour, the infection had already begun to spread.

"What did you do?" said Rupert. "How did you do that? Wait! I remember you now! You're a vampire — you attacked me in my cave! It's all coming back! This place is infested with the undead! God bless us all!"

"The police will have no problem believing he

A MEETING OF MINDS

thinks he killed a ghost," said Penny. "He sounds crazy."

"He is, I fear," said Gladys. "All those years of drink and drugs, and all that time in prison where drugs are as accessible as they are out here has affected his mind."

Penny looked up. "Granny! What about Mavis? She knew we came here a few days ago, and you told her she was going to play the organ at your wedding — you told her she was better than Ethel. She'll tell the police when she hears about Ethel's murder."

"And I shall tell Mavis and the police that I gave Ethel another chance to prove herself. Mavis knows how fickle I am, she'll understand," said Gladys. "Anyway, she's still got the wedding gig, she'll be happy enough."

Barney reached for his radio. "Okay. Is everybody ready? I'm going to call it in. Gladys, take Ethel's body out of stasis, and everybody try and look at least a little shocked — you *just* found a woman's body, remember. I'll tell them I'm here because I came with you to listen to Ethel play, after all it is a family wedding, and I'm on my break. They'll understand."

"Wait," said Gladys. She put her hand on Barney's arm. "Before you radio this in, we need to talk. Something feels very unfair about this whole thing — the cover up, and everything that went on thirty years ago. You're going to need to speak to a few people, Barney, and get a few strings pulled. It's only right. I'm finding it hard to think about Rupert going to prison for murder again. It wouldn't be fair. Will you help, Barney?"

Barney took his hand off his radio. "I said I'd help when all this started, Gladys. Tell me what you've got in mind, and I'll see what I can do."

CHAPTER NINETEEN

Gladys stepped off the *Water Witch* and smiled at the congregation. She knew she looked good, but the admiring glances she drew bolstered her confidence. Penny had moored the boat in the perfect position, and the beautification spell she had cast over the whole area had ensured the little pier looked as magnificent as the chapel she was about to get married in.

White roses had entwined their stalks around the handrails, and two white doves had heeded her magical call, and positioned themselves — one on each balustrade, their beaks aimed at the blue sky in an ornithological salute.

Gladys took a sniff of the rose tinted air and smiled once more at her admirers. They would lead her along the path to the chapel, where Charleston was patiently awaiting his bride. The sweet notes of organ music echoed through the valley, and Gladys gladly took the arm of her son as he approached her, his purple silk cravat the perfect match for his bright orange crushed velvet suit.

Penny, Willow, and Maggie stepped off the boat behind her, and Gladys gave them each a smile. They looked wonderful in matching dresses, and Gladys was happy she'd allowed Maggie to wear lavender, and not black as she'd planned.

She couldn't have asked for more beautiful bridesmaids, and she allowed herself a moment of pride for the family she'd produced.

Gladys had chosen her own outfit well, she'd decided, and nobody had mentioned the dramatic overnight weight loss which had allowed her to fit into such a curve hugging white dress. The spell would wear off by the next day, but Gladys didn't mind. She wasn't a vain woman, and she liked having a little meat on her derrière — it made sitting down far more comfortable.

Gladys gripped her bouquet tight in both hands. The colourful dried flowers gave her outfit a natural look, and the additional flowers dotted throughout her hair stood out beautifully against her freshly dyed blue perm.

As far as Gladys could tell, everybody who'd received an invitation was present, and she nodded her appreciation as the crowd clapped and cheered her arrival.

The gentle spell she'd imbibed the whole area with would put thoughts of Ethel's murder out of their minds for the day. When they awoke the next morning, they could begin the gossiping and speculation that always followed any crime in a small town. For today though, Gladys wanted only happy thoughts surrounding her.

"Are you ready, Mother?" said Brian, his arm a solid support in hers.

"I am," said Gladys. "I've never been more ready for anything."

Brian began walking, and Gladys matched his stride, keeping in step with her son as the rest of the congregation fell in behind them, following the mother and son along the pathway.

Gladys sighed as she rounded the final bend in the path and saw the chapel. She'd known her spell had been good, but the beautification magic had far surpassed her expectations. The white stone walls reminded her of Greek buildings, and the stained glass windows popped with colour, burnished by a golden sun. It was everything Gladys could have asked for, and she wished her mother could have been there to share in her happiness.

As Barney saw them approaching, he came to greet them, his suit fitting perfectly, with not a sliver of sock to be seen between his trouser hems and his shiny shoes. "You look stunning, Gladys," he said. "Charleston can't wait to see you."

"Is he okay?" said Gladys. "His head, I mean. He hasn't got headaches or anything, has he?"

Barney smiled. "He's fine. Honestly."

"You didn't let him know I told you, did you?" said Gladys.

"Of course not," said Barney. "Now, just concentrate on continuing to look so beautiful while I get everybody seated."

"And Inspector Jameson?" said Gladys. "Did you speak with him?"

"Yes, Gladys," said Barney. "I told you I would. He's on his way back from Scotland, and he's going to speak with Lady Green as soon as he gets back. Enough of that. You're here to get married. Not to worry."

He lowered his head, and Gladys smiled as he kissed her cheek. He was a fine young man, and she was happy that Penny had found him. "Thank you, Barney," she said.

A MEETING OF MINDS

Barney began leading the crowd of people into the chapel, and Gladys smiled as the photographer weaved between them, taking random pictures as she'd asked him to. Gladys wasn't photogenic, she knew that, and she always seemed more natural in photographs she wasn't aware had been taken. Of course, she'd pose for photographs with Charleston, but she was certain she'd shine brighter in the candid snapshots.

When the congregation had entered the chapel, Gladys looked around at her little posse. Her son, daughter, and grandchildren were her whole life, but she wished that Eva could be there too. They had their disagreements, sure — but there was nothing stronger than the bond between bickering sisters, and Gladys made a silent promise to herself that she'd see Eva more often in the future.

Birds sang as the organ music stopped briefly, and as the next notes burst into life, Brian squeezed Gladys's arm. "That's our cue, Mother," he said.

Mavis played beautifully, and as *Here Comes The Bride* burst from the open chapel doors, as bright and cheery as the day itself, Gladys allowed herself to be led inside by her first born.

If the beautification spell had done wonders for the outside of the chapel, it had performed miracles for the interior. The white rose theme continued inside, and the air smelt of fragrant petals and polished wood. Gone were the broken pews for the time being, being renewed to their former dark oak glory, dappled in the vibrant light which streamed through the colourful windows.

Gladys paused in the entrance, and Brian stopped alongside her. She closed her eyes and said a silent eulogy for Ethel, hoping the poor woman was at peace, and promising her that had she still been alive, it would have been her sitting at the organ.

When Gladys opened her eyes, she put all thoughts of the dead from her mind and concentrated on the living. Particularly Mavis, who seemed to be over egging her performance, her head bobbing, and her spine twisting as her fingers hammered out the notes. The notes *were* perfect though, and Gladys didn't begrudge her the time in the spotlight. She took a deep breath and turned her full attention to the man at the end of the aisle, the man who had agreed to accept her with all her many faults. The man she never thought she'd be fortunate enough to meet.

Charleston stood tall and proud, his suit immaculate, and his face a handsome reflection of the same love that Gladys felt for him. He licked his lips, and

Gladys smiled, her heart beating too fast, and her legs becoming jelly beneath her.

She ignored the admiring glances she drew as she navigated the aisle, and as Brian brought them to a gentle halt in front of the altar, she gave her son's hand a gentle squeeze. "Thank you, darling," she said. "I love you." She looked over her shoulder at her bridesmaids. "I love you all."

Mavis stopped playing and the chapel fell silent. The ceremony wasn't to be religious, and a registrar took the place of a vicar, his hair a mass of thick black curls and his face open and kind. He cleared his throat and looked out over the congregation."Today is to be a true meeting of minds," he began. "Between two people who have promised to support and love one another. The love they hold in their hearts is…"

Gladys zoned out, she watched the registrar's mouth, and she was aware of his words, but she didn't need to be told how she felt. She *knew* how she felt, and as Brian released her arm, and Charleston took her hand in his, she focused on preventing the brimming tears of joy from ruining her mascara.

WHEN *BLANKET STATEMENT* had finished their performance, and a DJ had taken over the duties of keeping the crowd entertained, Gladys surveyed the room. Michelle and Tony, the owners of *The Poacher's Pocket* hotel, had done the most amazing things with the big function room, and the food had been glorious.

As well as owning the hotel, Tony and Michelle also owned the cutting in the canal in which Penny's boat was moored. As Gladys watched her granddaughter drink another wine spritzer, she was relieved that the the *Water Witch* was only a short walk away, down a footpath. She didn't think either of her granddaughters would have managed a longer walk home.

Gladys and Charleston had entertained the guests with their first dance, and even Willow had seemed to enjoy *Fly Me To The Moon,* by Frank Sinatra. The Pimm's had run out quickly, and after the food had been served, and the cake cut, people had continued to enjoy the evening with plenty of wine, and lots of dancing.

Gladys squeezed her husband's hand. "How do you feel?" she said.

It was the first chance they'd had to be alone, and the little corner table they sat at was far enough from the speakers to make a conversation possible.

Charleston picked up one of the little origami

swans which had been placed on every table, and smiled at his wife. "I feel elated, Mrs Huang," he said. "I've never known such happiness."

"You know what I mean," said Gladys. She put a gentle hand on Charleston's head. "I mean up there. Do you feel okay?"

"I'm fine," said Charleston. "A little tired, but I'm fine. I promise."

"Another twenty minutes and I'm getting you back to The Haven," said Gladys. "It must be strange… knowing you can never come back to this world again."

"Everything I've ever wanted will be in The Haven with me," said Charleston, placing the paper swan in front of Gladys. "It'll be just me and my beautiful old bird."

"I'll take the beautiful, and possibly the bird," smiled Gladys. "But lay off the old!"

Charleston looked up. "Our privacy didn't last long," he said.

Gladys smiled at the approaching woman. She'd never apportion blame to what a woman wore, but surely Sharon knew that if she wrapped such a delightfully round bottom in such tight clothing, it was eventually going to attract the attention of a male or two.

Sharon stood beside the table. "Thank you both so much for inviting me," she said. "When Barney gave me the invite, I was a little taken aback — I don't think we've met before, have we?"

Gladys pulled out a seat, and Sharon sat down next to her. "Barney told me what fine work you do, and I'm a staunch supporter of the police. I always have been."

"Well I'm honoured to be here on your special day,' said Sharon, "and Barney tells me you made a generous donation to a local women's charity. That was very kind of you."

If Gladys concentrated hard enough, she could still feel the tingle in her palm that the slap she'd given Sharon had caused. "I'm all about helping women," said Gladys. "And I'm glad you've had a nice day."

Sharon began to stand up, but stared at Gladys, her eyes narrowing. "Those eyes of yours," she said. "They're so vivid. They remind of something I was certain I saw recently." She shook her head. "Ignore me," she giggled. "I've had too much Pimm's."

Gladys blinked, Sharon had indeed seen her eyes before. In the face of Inspector Jameson as the shape-shifting spell had faltered. "Get back to the dance floor," smiled Gladys. "Enjoy yourself while you're young."

When Sharon had left, Gladys took her husband's hand in hers. Their new rings twinkled as their fingers entwined, and Gladys stared at Charleston. "Are you ready, sweetheart?" she said. "I think it's time we got you back to the safety of The Haven. I don't want to tempt fate more than I have to, it's been very kind to me recently."

Charleston nodded. "I'm ready, Lady Huang. Its time to get you back to Huang Towers."

After saying their goodbyes, and before leaving, Gladys handed a thick envelope of money to Barney, with instructions as to who to give it to. "When you've paid Mavis and the band, keep the rest and spread it around between the family, including yourself," she said. "They're all too damned proud to take my money. It might be easier for them to take it from you."

Barney knew not to argue. He shook Charleston's hand, and kissed Gladys. "It was a lovely day," he said. "I'm so happy for you both."

"And remember what to say to Inspector Jameson, Barney," said Gladys. "It's important we do it properly."

Barney nodded. "I promise."

"Who's Inspector Jameson?" said Charleston.

"I'll tell you all about it when we get back to Huang Towers," said Gladys. "It's a long story. Now, fancy coming in the bathroom with me? We've got a portal to open."

CHAPTER TWENTY

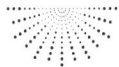

"*L*ady Huang?"

Gladys smiled. She'd been married for a month and still wasn't tired of being known as a Lady. She turned to face the voice. "Yes, Maria?"

The pretty little fairy hovered in the doorway, her silver wings a blur and her whole body aglow with bright light. Gladys had liked the idea of servants, but after only a few days of being waited on hand and foot, she'd become embarrassed of having things done for her which she knew she was capable of doing herself. To her surprise, and pride in the fact she must be a wonderful employer, all the servants had practically begged to remain in her employ. Gladys had relented, but insisted that the term *servant* be changed to the more endearing term of *Friend of the Family Huang*.

"Your guests are here, Lady Huang," said Maria. "They arrived in the portal room a few minutes ago. Should I direct them to the dining room?"

"If you wouldn't mind, Maria. That would be awfully kind of you. Tell them Charleston and I will be along shortly," said Gladys.

Maria bowed. A gesture of respect which Gladys had attempted to phase out, but was secretly pleased remained in place. Not all *Friends of the Family Huang* insisted on bowing, but the fairies in particular seemed to enjoy the tradition, and Gladys was appreciative of their respect.

When Maria had fluttered from the room, Gladys made her way to the balcony. The master bedroom looked out over the lake, and Charleston enjoyed nothing more than smoking a cigar while watching the scarlet patterns the setting sun made on the water's surface. With a strict no smoking indoors policy in place, Charleston was forced to enjoy his cigars al fresco, but Gladys knew he didn't mind. "Charleston," she said, peering through the wind ruffled muslin curtain. "Stub that stinky stick out, they're her. Grub's about to be served. We're having burgers and fries."

There was only so much venison and quail's eggs that Gladys could stomach, and it hadn't taken more than a week of her being a Lady before she'd instructed the chefs to produce less pretentious meals. One of the chefs, a troll named Herbert, made fries to die for, and Gladys knew that if ever The Haven and the mortal world were to merge, Hebert would find his fortune in a fast-food restaurant chain.

Charleston turned to face Gladys, and smiled. He flicked the cigar to the marble flagstones and stubbed it out under his shoe. "Desert?" he said.

"Knickerbocker glory. Brian's favourite. He's on a diet, so I've asked the chefs to include plenty of fruit."

"Delicious," said Charleston. He approached Gladys and hooked his arm through hers. "Allow me to escort you, Lady Huang. Our family awaits."

Gladys pushed him away. "I'm not a trophy wife, you daft old sod. They'll think I've gone soft if I saunter into the dining room hanging off your arm like a lovesick teenager."

Charleston laughed, the lines beneath his eyes softening, and his mirth echoing across the valley. "Have it your way, you miserable old boot. Anyway, if either of was a trophy spouse, you know that would be me."

Brian pushed the empty ice-cream glass away from himself, and loosened his shirt. "Delicious," he said. "And I don't feel guilty. I've had my five-a day."

Gladys looked around the table. Everybody seemed satiated, even Maggie, although she *was* eyeing up the cheese platter near Gladys's elbow. She slid it towards her daughter. "Cheese, darling?" she enquired.

"Just a sliver," said Maggie, spearing a half wheel of stilton on the end of the cheese fork. "I don't want to have nightmares."

Gladys removed the serviette from her lap and placed it on the table. She looked at Barney. "Now it's time for business," she said. "What news have you got?"

"It's good news," said Barney. "Everything went to plan."

"Rupert will spend a few years in a secure hospital," said Penny, "but that's better than spending another thirty years in prison."

Gladys couldn't have agreed more. The more she'd thought about the whole terrible situation, the more she couldn't help thinking about the part Ethel had played in it. Yes, Gladys was aware that the poor woman had been injured by Rupert all those years ago, but she was also aware that Ethel had known a man was incarcerated for a crime he hadn't committed. There had been wrong doing on both sides.

When Rupert actually *had* murdered Ethel, he'd not been of sound mind. Inspector Jameson had agreed, and when Barney had informed him he'd broken into his safe and found the file implicating him in a cover-up, Inspector Jameson had done the right thing. He could have denied everything — Gladys knew that. The file had been destroyed by tea, and Inspector Jameson could have walked away with his hands seemingly clean, but he hadn't, and Gladys had guessed he wouldn't. She'd sensed he was a good man from the first moment she'd met him.

The inspector had spoken to Lady Green, and between them they'd pulled enough strings to prevent Rupert from going to jail. A secure mental institute may have seemed as harsh as a cell, but with Brian being appointed as one of his therapists, Rupert would be well enough to convince the parole board he was ready for release as soon as he'd done enough time to satisfy the public appetite for justice.

"And my chapel?" said Gladys.

"Torn down," said Willow. "Just how you wanted. The last memories those walls held were happy ones of your wedding day. Penny and I are going to plant a few white rose bushes in its place. We thought it would be nice."

"It will, dear," said Gladys. "Both for Ethel, and for me."

"And as I promised," said Charleston, pouring brandy into his glass. "There will be a place for Rupert here in The Haven when he's been released. Everybody deserves a second chance, and I fear the mortal world is not a kind place for a man like Rupert. He'll fit in here just fine."

"He will indeed," said Gladys. "And he'll be treated in the way a man should be when he's paid his penance and been rehabilitated — fairly and without prejudice."

Gladys picked up a piece of burger as loud barking approached the dining room. "Bonnie!" she called. "Come and get it!"

The little dog bounded into the room, skidding on the hard wood floor. She ran to the table and sat obediently next to Gladys's chair, where she waited patiently, giving Gladys her paw before being allowed the treat.

Gladys watched the little dog as she devoured the morsel, then looked around the table once more. "Life's not bad is it?" she said. "Bad things happen, but look at us — a happy family who love each other. I don't understand how Lady and Lord Green could have done what they did to their son, but as long as we remain loyal to each other, both here in The Haven, and in the other world, we'll do just fine. I'm sure."

"Are you drunk, Granny?" said Penny.

Gladys smiled. "Not drunk, darling. Just happy and proud. It's an intoxicating mix."

Gladys and Charleston stood hand in hand with Bonnie between them, watching the family stepping one by one through the portal. Before Penny stepped through, she turned around. "You make a lovely couple," she said. "I hope you enjoy your trip."

"We will," said Gladys. "It'll be just me, Charleston, and Bonnie for a few weeks."

"And Boris," said Charleston. "You promised. You said it would be as much my honeymoon as it is yours. And I want to take him! Boris would love a trip around The Haven. You know he would — he's an inquisitive goat beneath that greedy exterior."

Gladys winked at Penny. "Okay, darling, Boris can come too."

He couldn't, but Gladys knew when to pick her battles. She'd cross that bridge when she came to it.

Penny smiled. "Happy honeymoon," she said, before turning to face the portal."

"We'll be back in time for Christmas!" shouted Gladys, as her granddaughter stepped into the light. "You're all to come here to celebrate it, okay? It will be fun!"

As the portal fizzled out and died, Gladys placed her head on Charleston's shoulder, and sighed. "I'm a lucky woman," she said. "A very lucky woman."

Charleston put his arm around his wife. "And I'm a lucky man," he said. "A lucky man indeed."

The End

Want more? Sign up for my mailing list here and be notified when a new book is published!

ABOUT THE AUTHOR

Sam Short loves witches, goats, and narrowboats. He really enjoys writing fiction that makes him laugh — in the hope it will make others laugh too!

Printed in Poland
by Amazon Fulfillment
Poland Sp. z o.o., Wrocław